SHE

Connects

SHE *Connects*

ISBN 978-3-907328-51-4

Bose Creative Publishers (BCP)

BCP is a collaborative publishing platform for writers, artists, poets, and changemakers. Profits from book sales support social causes. Books are available as e-books and as print copies in various online stores. Read more about our books and our volunteers on our website.

Website: www.bosecreativepublishers.ch
Social media: @bosecreativepublishers
Contact: bosecreativepublishers@gmail.com

SHE Writers Group

The She Writers Group believes in creative activism and has more than 45 women of Indian origin worldwide participating in this book project. Coming from diverse professional backgrounds, these women have come together to write and give a creative platform to women's voices. They have published five books of short stories and one poetry. Books published include *She Speaks* (short stories, 2018), *She Reflects* (flash fiction, 2021), *She Celebrates* (short stories, 2021), *Emotions in Rhythm* (poems, 2021), *She Shines* (short stories, 2022), *She Seeks* (short stories, 2023), *She Achieves* (short stories, 2024), and *She Connects* (short stories, 2025).

Join the *SHE Writers* on Social Media

Facebook: www.facebook.com/SHE.Writersfb
Instagram: @she_writingsbyindianwomen
Youtube: http://bit.ly/SHE-Writings

SHE Connects

Acknowledgements

Coordinators:
Dr. Vinita Godinho, Australia
Ms Bidisha Chakraborty, USA

Editors:
Ms. Debaleena Mukherjee, India
Dr. Rejina Sadhu, Switzerland
Ms. Saleha Singh, Australia (Copy-editing Lead)
Dr. Teesta Ghosh, USA (Editor-in-Chief)

Publishing:
Ms. Brindarica Bose, Switzerland

Thank you, SHE Team, for your collaboration!

SHE Connects

INTRODUCTION

She Connects is the seventh book of short stories published by 16 women authors of Indian origin from different parts of the world. Hailing from different professional backgrounds, the *SHE* project aims to provide a creative platform for women's voices and reflections on daily life. None of the authors come from a 'purely literary' background, yet as scientists, bankers, academics, engineers, managers, and home-makers, they all have a story to share.

The books in the *SHE* series revolve around a specific theme or genre. In the past, the themes have included stories woven around women's voices (She Speaks 2019), Indian festivals (*She Celebrates 2020; relaunched in 2021)*, flash fiction was the genre of choice in (*She Reflects, 2021*), stories of women belonging to marginal groups *(She Shines 2022)*, mystery and nostalgia *(She Seeks 2023), She Achieves (2024)* is a varied collection of short stories and flash fiction addressing women and work, and *She Connects (2025)* is based on unusual relationships.

Relationships, it goes without saying, sustain us from the moment we are born until our last breath. Some of these relationships are familial, others social, and still others professional. Some are fleeting, and others are long-lasting. The range of emotions that these relationships evoke can be positive, such as loyalty, duty and love, or negative where competitiveness, jealousy and rancour become predominant. Whatever its nature, all relationships are based on some sort of mental or emotional connection.

The authors of *She Connects* have shined a spotlight on the myriad ways in which unusual relationships are forged. Here is a preview of the stories contained in this book. In pre-Independence India large extended families relied implicitly on domestic

8

help/servants to run the household who then became an integral part of that family despite class barriers; in post- Independence India a little girl from a middle-class background is befriended by a man hailing from less advantaged socio-economic circumstances and remains her steadfast loyal supporter until the end of his life (*Pratapa and Punnu; Ondra Kannan*).

Singular friendships are cemented while navigating the ups and downs of life, whereas others are norm defying in an extraordinary way (*The Soul Sisters; Sakha! O Filos Mou!*). Even a seemingly antagonistic relationship can change to one of affection and mutual support under circumstances (*A Free Spirit*). Sometimes chance meetings at a grocery store, an airport lounge or in a remote place far from home can lead to deeply meaningful interactions that resonate deeply or even change the direction of one's life (*The Moonlit Clouds, The Circle of Life; The Messenger*). The influence of the departed on us mortals is not to be questioned, but simply accepted as part of the human experience

(*Robidadu; Once Upon a Holiday*). When all seems to be lost and one is floundering, connecting to a painting recognized as a masterpiece or even a wall clock can open the doors to salvation (*The Golden Embrace; Tick Tock*). And how can we forget our magical relationships with animals - a little girl's pet tortoise and an old lady's dog exemplify joie de vivre and steadfast loyalty (*The Girl and the Tortoise; Aaheli*). The most powerful relationship that one can have though is ultimately with oneself, the past self can guide the present self through difficult circumstances (*Around the Corner*).

The protagonists of these stories surely display a lot of grit, resilience and ingenuity. But above all they are risk-takers who step outside the bounds of conventional relationships to trust, connect and embrace change. We invite you dear readers to step into the world of unusual relationships to rediscover your own unique stories of connection.

We have been steadfast in our goal to support organisations that work for women and children. In

SHE Connects

2024, we held community outreach events in the United States and India to showcase the *SHE* series of books published by *Bose Creative Publishers*. We are encouraged by the conversations we sparked and the positive feedback we have received from our readers. In the future, we will explore new creative ways to spread our message of women's empowerment on different platforms.

We collaborate across many countries to publish a book of short stories about women annually on International Women's Day. We thank our authors, editors, and coordinators for persevering to bring this book to fruition despite unexpected challenges. Please visit us at *www.bosecreativepublishers.ch* and follow us on our social media handles *(@SHE.Writersfb, @shewritersig)*. To learn about what we do and our projects, and *www.bosecreativepublishers.ch* for our previous books and mission.

Editorial team: Debaleena Mukherjee, Rejina Sadhu, Saleha Singh, and Teesta Ghosh (Editor-in-Chief).

SHE Connects

SHE Connects

Table of Contents

SHE Connects

PARTAPA
AND PUNNU

SHUKLA LAL, INDIA

'Subhadra, how many times must I tell you to cover your face when the menfolk enter the kitchen?' said the sister-in-law to her newly married *bhabhi* (brother's wife).

'*Ji, Beji*,' answered the flustered young bride as she quickly pulled her sari over her head, wiping her sweaty brow with one hand while taking the fluffed-up *chapati* off the griddle.

This was the daily drama Partapa saw as he served the men of the house their meals in the kitchen.

Subhadra, my paternal grandma, was a pampered 14-year-old when she married. As was the custom in wealthy Punjabi homes, Partapa, a 10-year-

15

old lad, was sent as a domestic helper, or *mundu,* along with her dowry. The *mundu* was like a go-between who would relay everything about the treatment in her new home to the bride's family. He was also her confidante. Those were the days when young daughters-in-law were in *purdah.* Their job was to cook and produce children—an affinity developed between Partapa and Dadi.

'Don't cry, *behenji.* You will get used to purdah and cooking. Fortunately, this is a small family. Beji is tough but is also a woman. Think of her as your mother. Now, this is your home. Adapting to your in-laws´ way of life is your only means to be happy. I am here to support you.'

'Partapa became like my brother,' she told me later. 'I would share my problems with him. I told him I hated covering my face, especially when cooking in summer. Or how your grandpa's sister's authoritarian stance would make me very nervous. Without my knowledge, Partapa would relay my discomfiture to my parents. When they asked me how my in-laws treated me, I always answered that I was happy.'

Both my grandparents belonged to Amritsar. By the age of 15, Dadi became the mother of a son, my father. Dadi would calculate my father's age by reminding us that it was the landmark year of the Durbar, held in Delhi that signified India as a prosperous colony of England. Girls were only taught the Devnagri script at home by a Panditji to be able to read the holy books of Ramayana, Mahabharata, and Bhagavad Gita.

Life flowed on, and soon, there were six children. Through it all, Partapa was her pillar. He was now middle-aged and the cook of the family. He listened to her concerns as they underwent all the ups and downs of business and health. She saw that her sons and daughters both received the maximum education: Bachelor of Arts (BA) degrees for the girls and Master of Arts (MA) degrees for the boys in English medium. My father got married by 21, and soon, the two-storied house resounded with the pitter-patter of children's feet. Partapa was ageing when my parents left Amritsar for Ambala, but Dadi decided to send him along. She knew she could trust him to help my mother settle into a new city with her young family.

'I have decided to employ a *mundu*, Punnu, a Garhwali boy of 15 from Partapa's village, to help me and the elderly Partapa,' my mother, Biji, told my father, Pitaji, after a few months.

So Punnu joined our household when I was 4 years old. As time passed, Pitaji was transferred to Lahore, the headquarters of the British firm he worked for. Punnu and Partapa bonded well into our lives. While she relied on Partapa implicitly, Biji maintained a slight formality, as did he. Punnu soon became my mother's right-hand man.

We lived in a bungalow with a kitchen outside the house and separate quarters for staff. Partapa never entered the house, but Punnu was always in and out to fetch and carry. Punnu's duties included travelling with

Pitaji as his attendant on his tours. He was family, yet an employee who knew his limits. His loyalty was unquestionable.

'Punnu, bring my wallet,' Pitaji would instruct him often. Or, Biji would call out, 'Punnu, pay him from the money kept for household expenses,' when we children got buttered buns out of a black box tied on the breadman's cycle.

He often babysat us while my parents went to see a film. We were given a four-anna silver coin and carrot *halwa* as a treat. Punnu looked after the coin while he played with us before putting us to bed.

'*Bibiji*, here is the four anna coin,' he'd say the following day. When Partapa became feeble and had to be retired, Punnu became the pillar of our lives. A silent trust and a mysterious, respectful bond had developed between him and Biji.

'*Bibiji*, my wife has sent a message that the roof of my house has fallen. I will have to go home.' Punnu would ask for help only when he had an emergency in his home. Biji immediately sent him home with enough cash and rations to rehabilitate the family.

Once, while helping my father put on his coat before he left for the office, my mother asked him, 'Do you ever count the money in your coat pocket or wallet?'

'No, you are here, and on tour, Punnu looks after me,' he answered.

'Okay then, whenever I find any loose notes or coins in your pockets, they are mine,' she laughed. Over time, my mother began to save notes and coins as her secret savings, in addition to what she had put away from the household accounts.

By 1946, the Independence movement had taken a serious turn. Schools closed before the summer holidays, and we were urged to leave Lahore. We didn't believe it and went to Shimla for an extended summer holiday instead. Punnu and our new cook joined us. By then, Punnu was a trustworthy, loyal family member who was quiet and efficient. Biji was so intuitive to her needs in looking after a big family. He seemed to know when she was troubled, when to herd us children away or when she needed a cup of tea.

By the end of October 1946, Lahore was on fire. Partition occurred on 15 August 1947, and we never returned to Lahore. We moved all over India with our helpers. Finally, the company's head office shifted to Calcutta. En route, my parents left my sister and me in Amritsar to save our lost years in school. Due to our fluent English, we got a triple promotion! Punnu left behind a small steel box in my Dadi's safe custody.

One day, my mother wrote to my aunt in Amritsar to open Punnu's box.

'But why?'

'I will write the details later,' answered Biji.

The helper had to carry it on his head from the storeroom as it was so heavy. When the lock was broken and the lid lifted, our eyes opened wide with surprise. 'Oh my God! It's a sight to behold!' My Dadi, aunt and I said in one voice.

It was full of coins and notes shoved in between his clothes. The fabric was like old flaking paper in our hands with the weight of the coins. We were shocked! He was our loyal and trusted Man Friday, who had seen us through hard and good times. His village home was the envy of his relatives, as he had told my parents with gratitude. They had given him whatever was needed to build it and a yearly bonus for his family. He saw us growing up, as we had seen him grow from a *mundu* to a grown-up young man.

My aunt told my mother that it was Ali Baba's tiny treasure. What should we do with it?

'Keep it for the girls' *tonga* (horse buggy) fare to school,' she responded. 'Punnu has become street smart. The big city has influenced him.'

'One day, I caught him taking notes from your brother's coat. When he saw me staring at him in disbelief, he froze, his face red. The many years of trust vanished in thin air as his embarrassed eyes met mine. Before he left, I reminded him about his box in

Amritsar. He said he would pick it up on his way home. But don't worry, he is too ashamed that he won't come back.'

We were aghast, yet sorry, too. My mother was right. He never came to collect his trunk. We still remember Punnu with affection. My mother's words, too, helped remove any malice towards him.

'I can't help feeling betrayed. I trusted him like a son and tried to fulfil all his needs. To know Punnu had become a sneak, is heartbreaking. Yet we must forgive him. Our bond of many years cannot be erased just like that.'

Note from the Author: There are mystical relationships between humans. This autobiographical tale is about the relationship between domestic employers and employees. Sometimes, it remains after the old retainers age and retire from the same family. A very affectionate bond develops within a social formality. They know the family intrigues and the nature of each member better than the family itself! They have to be discreet and can cause immense trouble or bring their earthy wisdom to ease the tensions.

It's the mystical luck of the draw.

THE SOUL SISTERS

VINITA GODINHO, AUSTRALIA

Research shows it is likely that each one of us has a look-alike somewhere in the world, although the probability of actually meeting them is remote. There's even a 'Doppelganger theory' about biologically unrelated look-alikes or doubles of a living person.

A firm believer in scientifically verifiable evidence, I would have been tempted to brush these claims off as yet another kooky idea, had I not witnessed the strange but true story of the unique relationship between two childhood friends—let's call them 'Earth' and 'Water'—the soul sisters. They would have met as four-year-olds in a famous Kolkata convent, as nursery students on their first day of school. Yet neither has any conscious memory of this, as they were assigned to separate sections that only met at playtime. The old black-and-white class photos from this time show the two little girls in their starched uniforms, nervously looking up at the camera, possibly wondering when they could get back to the safety of their mothers' arms.

It wasn't until the sections were reshuffled a few years later that the two girls were in the same class, but even then, their paths did not cross initially. Earth was an active, sports-loving chatterbox who ran off to the basketball court at every opportunity, while Water was a quiet and sickly child, more likely to be found in the library, lost in the world of books. Their first conscious memory of each other was when Water, recovering from a long illness, was randomly assigned a seat next to Earth. A kind-hearted soul, Earth took Water under her wing to bring her up to speed with the lessons she had missed, soon discovering that they had a lot in common, including to everyone's surprise—even their classmates and teachers who had never noticed it before - their looks.

The two became best friends, and like little girls everywhere, were soon inseparable at school and home. Both girls had similar backgrounds and a sibling each, yet their bond seemed stronger than their blood ties.

As the teenage growth hormones kicked in, even their mothers were taken aback at how closely Earth and Water now resembled each other. They were of similar height and build and had the same hairstyle and mannerisms, including tone and voice—so much so that they were often mistaken for each other at school. Soon, people started referring to them as 'the twins.' Their teachers were even more puzzled upon realising that their handwriting was very similar, and they often scored the same test marks. Unbeknownst to the girls, some teachers began to question whether there was a possibility that the girls were copying from each other, so to the chagrin of the besties, they were separated and assigned seats on opposite ends of their classroom. Yet, as the year passed, with the girls seated as far from one another as possible, nothing changed, and they continued to score similar marks. They were now also sharing extracurricular interests, with Water testing her throw ball skills and Earth spending more time reading. Both participated in the end-of-year talent show (Earth joined the classical dancers and Water the choir) and were elected by their peers as house monitors. As the girls' friendship was obviously encouraging them to blossom and grow, their teachers finally acknowledged their 'twinning' as a positive influence, and gave up trying to separate Earth and Water.

The years sped by, captured in photos as the girls progressed from school to higher secondary studies (called 'Plus-two' in those days)—still together, supporting one another to do their best. Their classmates and teachers were now used to thinking of them as a package deal, with the rare exceptions being the sports field, where Earth excelled, and the school band, where Water was the lead singer.

This charming twin existence was first tested when the two girls studied at different universities. Each strongly felt the other's absence as they had to forge new friendships and learn new skills without the comfort of each other's support. Yet they managed to stay connected, braving the unreliable Kolkata telephones and buses (email and social media would not be on the horizon for decades!) to keep in touch between lectures, exams, and their first romantic relationships. Earth graduated first, landing a job with a large multinational, while Water studied further before entering the corporate world. Yet, their paths continued to intertwine, and their circle now widened to include their partners, who—it goes without saying—also shared similar natures, interests, and career paths.

The next chapter in their story saw the friends branching further out, moving to different cities as the responsibilities of work and married life took priority. Yet both would admit that despite not seeing each other as often, they somehow always knew when the other was feeling down, and a quick phone call was all it took to reconnect and help them untangle whatever mess they were facing. The advent of social media made it easier for the soul sisters to share the ups and downs of their everyday lives and offer reassurance, advice, recipes, or just silly jokes to stay connected.

Would it surprise you then to know that over the years, Earth and Water's personal and professional lives continued to follow a similar trajectory—to the point where if one had a life-changing experience, the other expected that sooner or later, they would experience it too? When one moved overseas with their family a few years later, the other also ended up unexpectedly moving to another continent. When one switched career paths to follow her passion, the other also reached a similar decision, taking a break from work to study. Could these different yet parallel experiences be put down to mere coincidence, or was there a more spiritual explanation to be explored, with similar souls independently making similar choices?

With time, as Earth and Water grew their circle of family and friends, criss-crossing across continents and workplaces, they kept weaving the precious threads of their unique friendship closer, remaining an essential part of the other's life story. Be it fair weather or storm, these soul sisters have now lovingly tended to their shared garden of life for more than five decades, finding ways to celebrate or commiserate together, no matter what life throws at them. Their photos, which now include partners, in-laws, and grown children who are also friends, are a testament to how the roots of one strong relationship can grow multiple offshoots, each providing ongoing support and nourishment for the other.

As I write this story, Earth and Water—still living on separate continents—are entering their sixth decade together, with retirement and grandchildren hovering on the horizon. Having celebrated this milestone year with their classmates on a nostalgic journey back to the Kolkata school where they first met, the soul sisters, named after their sun signs, are planning their next adventure together.

How do I know so much about their lives? Well, dear reader, I am fortunate enough to be one of this pair of soul sisters. I will let you guess which one!

ONDRA KANNAN

RADHIKA SINGH, INDIA

He had beautiful sea-green eyes flecked with gold. I never understood why my mother called him Ondra Kannan (the squint-eyed man). OK, as we called him was a merry young boy when we first met. He was one of those nameless, faceless people on the periphery of society who did everything they could to make our lives more comfortable in return for a few kind words, an occasional meal, some hand-me-down clothes, and a few rupees.

He must have been about 15 to my five—a 10-year age difference that felt massive at the time but seemed to shrink as we grew older. He doted on me, and I followed him everywhere, absorbing his life lessons like a sponge. He taught me to make a flower necklace without string, hold a kitten by the scruff of its neck, take (steal) flowers from someone's garden without getting caught, climb a tree, and scale a wall without scraping my knees. Not everything he taught me was strictly legal, but my mother, busy with her new baby, was grateful he kept me occupied. What she didn't know wouldn't hurt her, I thought. Most importantly, OK taught me to be happy in my own company.

We belonged to different worlds. My father worked for a multinational company, my mother was educated and polished, and my sister and I attended English-medium schools. We had family members in good positions, went on holidays, and lived a harmonious, everyday life. OK lived in a tiny tarpaulin-roofed room in a slum near Vivekananda Park in Kolkata. His mother was a tired-looking woman who seemed to be perpetually ill, his sisters were already working as live-in maids, and his father was a jobless drunkard. Despite the constant domestic violence at home, OK remained cheerful—a lotus in the squalid cesspool of that slum.

OK was a constant presence in our neighbourhood, doing odd jobs for everyone—putting up paintings, changing fuses, mopping floors, buying vegetables, and more. I often tagged along with him, chattering and asking hundreds of questions. He would listen carefully and answer patiently, explaining in words I could understand. He would take me along to meet his friends, too—ordinary, kind and generous people living day-to-day lives. They gathered me into their warm embrace and treated me with a warmth, love and affection that I rarely see in my social circle. I remember them so well, even now, after all these years. *Balai er Ma* (Balai's mother), a weary-looking old lady in a white sari always hugged me and found something for me to eat in her meagre kitchen. A *narkel naru*, an orange or maybe a *sandesh*. The love with which she fed me made them taste so significantly sweeter. Balai *da* himself, a self-proclaimed local thug or goon of sorts, would lift

35

me in his arms and swing me round and round till I was dizzy with joy.

Then there was Ganesh, who worked as a security guard in my school. He would never speak to me in school, but always had a secret smile for me. And, when we visited him in his one room on Purnadas Road, I would sit and play with the stray dog he allowed to sleep there while he played cards with OK and their other friends. He never objected to my presence, nor did I ever feel uncomfortable there. There were others: the tea shop man opposite Triangular Park, the homeless old man who lived by the corner fence of Vivekananda Park with his beloved dog Lalu, and Polly and Molly, sisters who worked as maids in one of the houses. Their professions, money and backgrounds made no difference to me then. The only thing that mattered was how kind, good and loving they were.

OK was wonderful with animals, instinctively knowing how to handle them with care. He was my first teacher, always patient, even when I cried over a dead kitten or puppy. He taught me that death was just another chapter in the book of life.

He had a mischievous side, too. Once, I saw him being yelled at by Sunny Uncle (so named after his pug, Sunny). OK meekly accepted the scolding, then stuffed a bunch of freshly bloomed dahlias into my satchel—flowers stolen from Uncle's garden for his sweetheart.

My parents discouraged our friendship as we grew older. Our meetings became infrequent and awkward, especially after we moved to a different locality when I was 12.

OK set up a tea stall near Lake Road, where I sometimes took friends. He listened discreetly to our teenage tales but never interfered, only once warning me about a boy involved in drugs. At 18, I joined a bank, working in their debt collection department—a tough job for a shy teenager. My 'beat' was South

Kolkata, starting at Kalighat and going to Lake Police Station, up Southern Avenue to Golpark and then back again to Gariahat and Desha-priya Park. It was a perfect square, teeming with credit card defaulters. I had a list and a 'collector' with me—a man who took the cash and issued receipts, but he dictated his terms, leaving me to convince people to pay. Needless to say, I was a miserable failure at this job, since no one took me seriously. I was a thin, almost scrawny teenager with no personality or authority. Credit defaulters were made of sterner stuff, and they could not be bothered enough even to let me state my issues. Things were looking bad for me.

One day, the collector and I ended up at OK's stall, where he listened to our hopeless, helpless conversation about being unable to meet our targets and the consequences. Things were looking grim, and I feared losing my job because of my inability to perform. That day, he stepped in. He took the collector aside and had a whispered conversation with him, which neither of them shared with me. The man turned and told me he was taking the next day off and that OK would join me on my collection visits instead.

I got there bright and early the next day. OK was waiting for me. He introduced me to a group of men in tight black t-shirts and blue jeans. To my youthful eyes, they looked strong and imposing. We began walking in a group, me in the centre, surrounded by them. People turned to stop and stare. It felt so good. I got a sense of what being powerful felt like that day.

We started our day at a sweet shop in Lake Market, and after that, people paid up without resistance. Neither OK nor his friends actually did anything. Everywhere we went, their mere presence, silent and imposing, standing behind me was enough. They did not need to say a word or even participate in the collection process. I was elated. That one day changed everything for me. My confidence had grown by leaps and bounds, and I could hold my own in very challenging situations after that. My collections improved, and so did my position in the workplace. My boss noticed and acknowledged my efforts. Soon, he transferred me to a department without fieldwork, where I excelled. OK's intervention had turned my career around. That was his style—never explicitly illegal, yet it always carried an edge of thrilling danger.

The years passed, and our meetings became rare. I once took my father to meet him, and we reminisced about the old days. OK, now greying and worn, still had those green-gold eyes and a hint of his merry smile. But things had changed. The pressures of real life had knocked away all traces of the carefree young man I had known and adored. I noticed a tremor in his hand as he poured the tea. Beads of sweat dotted his brow, and I could see that his smile did little to mask the unease simmering just beneath the surface. As I climbed the corporate ladder, got married, and became busy dealing with life, I lost touch with OK and barely thought of him. However, I subconsciously never forgot the lessons he taught me about being kind, helpful and being there for our friends.

One night, during a thunderstorm, a woman knocked on my door. She introduced herself as Kartik's wife. I didn't know who Kartik was, but since she was wet and shivering in the rain, I invited her in, made her comfortable by asking her to sit down, and gave her a towel and a glass of water. She took them gratefully and then sat quietly, catching her breath after what appeared to have been a long walk in the rain. It was only when the lights came back on, that I realised that the wetness on her face was not the rain but tears. She was crying, and shaking uncontrollably. I gently inquired what was wrong. Gradually, through her choked sobs, the story unfolded.

Finally, after 45 years, I learned Ondra Kannan's real name—Kartik Mondal. I also learned the depth of his affection for me—his wife knew everything about my life and achievements. She said that he thought of me as if I were the child they had never had, taking immense pride in my career and personal progress. He kept track of my life through social media, although he never sent a friend request. Every year on my birthday, he would bring home a cake, and they would both cut it together and share it with their neighbours.

The revelation of how much OK loved me, celebrating my achievements and birthday each year, filled me with shame and guilt for letting our bond lapse. I struggled to hold back my tears as she spoke.

OK had suffered a stroke and was lying in the corridors of the Calcutta Medical College. She had not been able to get him a bed. Doctors had said there was little hope of recovery. In her desperation, this humble woman, who had never met me, had braved the thunderstorm to find me and seek help.

We rushed to the hospital, battling fallen trees and blocked roads. When we arrived, we found familiar faces from Purnadas Road, aged and weathered by time but still recognisable, gathered in silent mourning. OK had passed away just before we got there.

At that moment, standing among those who had come to say goodbye, I realised the depth of my loss. OK had been more than just a friend—he was a part of my soul's fabric, woven into my childhood memories and beyond. His love was quiet but unwavering, a silent support I had taken for granted. He had followed my life from afar, rejoicing in my successes, never intruding but always caring. His wife's words, recounting how they celebrated my birthday each year, cut deep into my heart, making me painfully aware of his love and pride for me.

As I stood there, I felt the weight of all the unspoken words, the unexpressed gratitude, bearing down on my shoulders. I wanted to thank him for his lessons and for being my guide and protector. I wanted to apologise for not staying in touch or realising how much he meant to me sooner. But now, all I could do was promise to honour his memory and live with the same kindness and quiet strength he had shown throughout his life.

OK's modest and unpretentious life, though lived on the periphery of our world, was abundant in spirit and generosity. His essence was like those sea-green eyes flecked with gold—a rare and exquisite reflection of a soul that saw beauty and goodness in the simplest things. As I left the hospital, I realised that OK's legacy would live on in the way I chose to live my life, in the kindness I showed to others, and in the stories, I would tell of a man who taught me that love is not about grand gestures but the small, silent acts that touch the heart. The unusual relationship he and I shared will remain a shining reminder of how love can manifest in the most unexpected ways.

OK, my friend, teacher, and silent guardian—thank you for everything. Your spirit will always be a part of me, a quiet strength I will carry forward. Rest in peace, Kartick Mondal, knowing your love and lessons will never be forgotten.

Glossary

Ondra Kannan: Squint eyed man.
Balai er Ma: Balai's mother.
Narkel Naru: Popular Bengali sweet dish made of coconut and jaggery.
Sandesh: Popular Bengali sweet dish made of curdled milk and sugar.
Balai da: A respectful form of addressing an elder brother, here a person named Balai.

A FREE SPIRIT

Teesta Ghosh, USA

Churni scanned the brightening horizon from her perch on top of the overbridge. With its red and white colonial-era building and bustling platform, the Serai railway station lay like a postage stamp below her. The motley crowd of office goers, college students, and fruit and vegetable vendors were waiting to board the *Purvi* local. Churni picked out the MLA in his pristine *kurta-pajama* and mentally noted the precise position of the corpulent figure of Constable Hari Singh at the edge of the crowd.

She then narrowed her eyes and looked directly at the signal at the far end of the platform. The amber light had turned green, announcing the imminent arrival of the *Purvi* local. The train waited at the platform for exactly seven minutes, within which she had to execute her plan. Her right hand grasped for the pocket knife tucked inside the folds of her *dupatta* that encircled her slender waist. She was ready. She crouched, pushing her 12-year-old body through the narrow rails, and reached out for the rainwater drain pipe. With her tendril-like arms and legs entwined around the pipe, she slid down effortlessly and dropped onto the platform.

At that instant, the *Puri* 'local' thundered into the Serai railway station, setting off a mad scramble to get onto the train. Churni pushed through the swarming bodies and hoisted herself onto a compartment. It was packed to the rafters with commuters on their way to the big city. Churni spotted a balding man clutching an office bag in one hand and grasping the top rail with the other. The man had managed to doze off in these conditions. The outline of his bulging wallet was visible in his back pocket. Churni manoeuvred herself directly behind him, drew out the knife, flicked it open and made a horizontal cut on the fabric. The wallet silently dropped into her *dupatta*. She then quickly exited the compartment from the other door and jumped onto the rails. Picking herself up, she ran across the tracks and hoisted onto the other platform. She turned back briefly to see the train pulling out of the platform.

Churni ran swiftly and entered an abandoned shed at the far end of the platform. She stopped a minute to catch her breath, then squatting on the floor, gingerly lifted the wallet from inside her *dupatta* and overturned its contents. Five ten-rupee notes, a few coins, and some dried flowers wrapped in paper tumbled on the ground. She was relieved that there were no notes of large denominations because getting rid of them without arousing suspicion was difficult. After all, she was an orphan living on strangers´ kindness at the Serai railway station. She did not know how she ended up here, nor did it matter. All she knew was that this railway station that she was familiar with, like the back of her hand, was her home.

SHE Connects

As she carefully buried the notes inside her *kurta*, Churni felt hunger pangs gnawing within her. She debated her options: she could either get tea and bread from the tea stall run by Ramu or visit one of the innumerable shops selling savouries and sweets right outside the station. Churni decided to treat herself to a platter of *poori-bhaji* and *ladoo* today. But she had to be careful with the money. It had to be stretched out for at least a week before she pickpocketed another unwitting passenger.

Constable Hari Singh relaxed visibly once the 'up train' had left the station. The railway platform was somnolent except for a few stragglers and stray dogs that were roaming around. Hari Singh sauntered across to Ramu's tea stall on the platform for his mandatory *chai* and *biscuit*. There was nothing much to do in this small station of a small town until the *Purvi* local returned at 6:30 p.m. with passengers returning home from the big city. Today, the station master, Dayaram Babu, was also at Ramu's tea stall.

'*Namaste*! Dayaram babu,' said Hari Singh.

The generally mild-mannered station master looked somewhat perturbed today.

'Oh! Hari Singh! Just the person I wanted to meet.'

'Is something the matter, sir?'

'I got disturbing news from my supervisor. It appears that a gang is targeting daily commuters on trains. There are reports of stolen wallets, chains and watches. We must be vigilant here.'

'Don't worry, sir. I will be on high alert when the train arrives and departs Serai. Nothing and nobody can evade Constable Hari Singh.'

Hari Singh knew that the last sentence was a weak assurance at best. He was assigned to the Serai station by the head of the local *thana*. He expected this assignment to lead to promotions and plum assignments. But here he was, stuck at the same place and job, with his retirement age approaching rapidly. Whenever Hari Singh broached the subject of his promotion with his commanding officer, the man would gleefully point to his expansive middle and say, 'Hari Singh, you fail the annual fitness test every year. Can we have an unfit policeman serving the community?' This admonishment was doled out annually at the time of his performance review. Hari Singh promised to reduce his weight every year but failed miserably. The lure of plump *gulab jamuns*, *motichoor ladoos* oozing *ghee* and thick *jalebis* drenched in syrup, available in plentiful shops outside the station, proved to be his downfall.

If this was not enough to feel dispirited, another constable had recently been assigned to the Serai railway station. Constable Sundar Ram was a confident young bloke with a spring in his step. One day, when the MLA's all-important leather folio fell out of his hands while boarding the train, Constable Hari Singh picked it up and ran after the moving train to place it in the outstretched hands of the MLA. However, he had to give up, unable to propel his considerable girth forward. From the corner of his eye, he had seen Constable Sundar Ram sniggering and a gaggle of college-bound girls giggling. But as providence would have it, another opportunity to redeem himself was opening up.

Churni, her hunger pangs satiated, climbed to her perch on top of the overbridge in swift, fluid moves, using her arms and legs like a trapeze artist. She could now spend the next few days playing marbles with boys on the street or swinging from the branch of a *Gulmohar* tree. She was a free spirit and a sharpshooter rolled into one.

Then, as risk-prone and brash persons are prone to do, Churni got careless. It was a cloudy morning, and a drizzle had prompted the commuters to huddle even more tightly under the roof covering the platform. Churni looked down and did not spot

Constable Hari Singh anywhere. Churni was on the platform in a trice and hopped onto a compartment when the *Purvi* local stopped. A woman was trying to soothe her bawling baby and, in the process, had left her handbag unattended. Without wasting a moment, Churni picked up the bag, covered it partially with her *dupatta* and jumped off the train.

Following her usual action plan, Churni headed straight to the secluded shed. But that day, a surprise awaited her. Constable Hari Singh was on his way to the station when the sudden onset of the drizzle forced him to take cover in the shed. As luck would have it, Churni came face to face with the person she wanted to avoid.

'What are you doing here, Churni? And what are you doing with a ladies' handbag?' Before Churni could react, the constable had snatched the bag from her and had encircled her upper arm in a vice-like grip. Churni knew instantly that the game was up, and she had to think fast to extricate herself from the situation.

'I am poor. I must eat, you know...' said Churni said in a matter-of-fact tone.

'You are a thief, and I will put you in jail!' thundered Hari Singh.

Seeing her options disappearing, Churni played a card she thought could work.

'Listen, police *ji*. I have an idea. From now on, I will report all the misdeeds at the station if you let me go.'

Constable Hari Singh looked long and hard at Churni and contemplated what the girl had just proposed; what she offered made perfect sense to him. This girl could be his ticket to a promotion.

'I am letting you go this time...but remember...' he said, relaxing his grip. An unspoken pact had been struck between the ageing officer of the law and a 12-year-old waif who survived by committing petty crimes.

SHE *Connects*

The collaboration between Hari Singh and Churni began to yield results. Churni reported to Hari Singh that some ruffians from the town were harassing college girls at the station. She informed him that although Ramu, the tea stall owner, advertised that he used only 'pure or *asli*' products, Churni had seen him diluting the milk with water with her own eyes. Churni alerted Hari Singh about the nefarious auto-rickshaw drivers who were fleecing their customers by tampering with their meters. Constable Hari Singh started cracking down on the miscreants. Some were arrested, some fined, and others were let go with severe warnings. Suddenly, Hari Singh's superiors noted his excellent work, which he hoped would lead to a promotion.

Constable Hari Singh was pleased with Churni. If, on occasion, he looked the other way when she stole a wallet or two, he justified it on humanitarian grounds. 'The poor girl must eat. She has no one in the world,' he reasoned. Over time, an inexplicable bond began to grow between the unlikely pair. In the long afternoons, when the railway station looked deserted, Hari Singh would summon Churni to the spot under the *Gulmohar* tree, where he ate his lunch.

'Here, eat this,' he would say, offering her a portion of his *roti* and *sabzi*.

Churni would pepper him with questions while chomping on the *roti*.

'How can I become a police constable, just like you?' she would ask innocently.

'You must improve your character, Churni. A pickpocket cannot expect to be a police constable,' Hari Singh would point out the obvious to the girl.

'We are both working to fill our stomachs. What's the difference?' Churni would argue.

Exasperated, Hari Singh would say, 'Run along now. It's time for my nap.'

On other days, Hari Singh lectured her about what he called the wider world.

'There's a country called *Umrika*, where everything is done by machines—cooking, cleaning, washing clothes.'

'What's *Umrika*? Is it the village next to Serai?'

'It is very, very far. One has to travel by plane.' Hari Singh would show off his knowledge.

'You know why India cannot catch up with *Umrika*? It's because of people like you, Churni. Look at you; you don't know how to read or write. You are a *jungli!* He then would pat her head affectionately.

'I bet no one in *Umrika* can run or climb as fast as me.' Churni would retort, her sense of dignity pricked.

Then came the day when Hari Singh and Churni were thrust into the limelight most dramatically.

It all concerned the local MLA's pet goat – Lali. Lali, a pure breed Alpine goat, was the MLA's dear and prized possession. Rumour had it that the MLA had won three successive elections because he consumed goat milk. Elections were looming again, and precisely at this critical moment, Lali had stopped producing milk for some unfathomable reason. It was a crisis of grave proportions for the MLA. Therefore, the MLA had decided to take his goat by train to be checked out by a vet who was based in the big city. He arrived one morning at the Serai railway station with the goat and two attendants to board the *Purvi* local. Hari Singh was at the spot, supervising the surging crowd waiting to get on the train. The signal had turned green, which meant that the train would arrive at the station in four minutes. Churni was watching the drama unfolding below from her perch on the overbridge. What happened next would become part of the local folklore. Lali, unsettled by the commotion, tugged at the rope held by the attendant. The attendant tried to hang on to the rope, but it was too late. Lali had jumped from the platform onto the tracks. The poor animal then stood on the tracks, petrified, bleating its heart out. Pandemonium ensued. The MLA, besides himself, started shouting, demanding immediate action. All eyes were now on Hari Singh. Hari Singh yelled at Ramu, 'Run...tell Dayaram Babu to phone the driver to stop the train.' But the more significant predicament was getting the goat off the tracks. All eyes turned on Hari Singh. He was contemplating his next move when he found Churni next to him.

'I will get the goat off the tracks.'

'Don't ...you will get killed.'

Before Hari Singh could stop her, Churni got off the platform and planted herself beside the terrified animal. She tried to push Lali off the tracks, but the goat would not budge. 'It seems the hoof of her front leg has got trapped under the trestles,' shouted some-one. Churni abandoned her previous plan, took off her *dupatta,* and wrapped it around Lali's middle. Lying flat on the platform she passed the other end of the *dupatta* to Hari Singh. Then she bent down and extricated the trapped hoof. 'Pull! Pull!' Churni shouted at Hari Singh. With both of them pulling and pushing, Lali was finally airborne and landed safely on the platform. Churni clambered to the top to loud cheers from the crowd.

In due time, Constable Hari Singh got the much-coveted promotion. Many months had passed since the incident. It was early winter, and Churni, as usual, was on her perch on top of the overbridge. Suddenly, she heard Hari Singh and Dayaram Babu, the station master, call out to her excitedly from below. 'Come down Churni! We have news for you.' Churni scrambled down in her usual fashion. Both were speaking at the same time. The station master was waving a piece of paper at her. 'Look! The government of India has announced the National Bravery Awards for children for Republic Day. And your name is on the list, Churni, for exceptional bravery in rescuing an animal from certain death. What an honour. There's a cash reward of 10,000 rupees, too!!' Looking at Hari Singh and Dayaram Babu's beaming faces, Churni concluded that something good must have happened to her after all.

Glossary

Purvi: eastern.
MLA: member of the Legislative Assembly.
Kurta-pajama: long tunic and loose trousers.
Dupatta: long scarf worn with tunic and loose trousers by Indian women.
Namaste: salutation or greeting in Hindi.
Chai: tea.
Roti-sabzi: wheat bread and a vegetable dish.
Gulmohar: a tree with bright orange blossoms.
Gulab Jamun: Indian dessert soaked in sugar syrup.
Jalebi: Fried Indian dessert.
Motichoor ladoo: a spherical Indian dessert.
Jungli: wild.
Thana: police precinct.

TARA'S STELLAR LIFE

SALEHA SINGH, AUSTRALIA

'Wake up, *Baba*. I'm here,' she whispered, her eyes were dry, but a typhoon raged inside her. She knew the finality of her words. How many times had she whispered these words to him when he was having a nightmare—moaning and thrashing in deep sleep? But today, he didn't move.

She looked around the small room, scanning faces she didn't recognise. *Baba* was well-loved, but this many people!

She remembered entering this room 25 years ago. It had not changed much, except for a photo of them in happier times on the wall at the foot of his bed.

It was a hot summer morning when the village *Pradhan* invited her to school, promising a special gift for academic excellence. She was about eight or ten— she didn't know her exact age, nor did her family. Excited, she wore her best clothes to receive the special gift. No one was there—only her and him.

'I called you early, so the other children aren't jealous of you receiving this special gift,' he said. He gave her colourful books and a red drink, which she drank in a gulp. She hadn't eaten that morning; school to home was an hour's walk, and with eight siblings, and only her father working, skipping meals was normal.

She woke up to an unfamiliar swaying motion. Confused, she looked around to unknown faces and scenery. Turning, she saw the *Pradhan*. 'It's okay,' he whispered. 'We're going to Pandeveshwar, where you will get more prizes.'

'But what about Ma and Abba?' she asked, realising she was on a train. An uncomfortable feeling knotted her stomach.

'Don't worry, I stopped by to tell them.' Relieved, she started to enjoy the first train journey of her young life. Pandeveshwar never came, and she was still on the train at nightfall. 'How much longer?' she asked. After the initial platitudes, the *Pradhan* ignored her. Too scared, she cried quietly, praying that her parents would find her. The passengers on the train looked away.

The following day, she was unceremoniously put on a *rickshaw* that transported her to the doorstep of an old house. Even in her innocence, she knew this wasn't a school. A woman opened the door and ushered them inside. Seeing a friendly face, she trusted the woman and followed her inside.

The house seemed huge—she, who was used to living in a two-room mud hut. She quickly scanned the place, seeing many more women and an older woman.

64

'Here, she is,' the *Pradhan* said.

'But she's a child,' the older woman said.

'You will not be disappointed,' the *Pradhan* smiled and left without a backward glance.

The older woman pulled her into an embrace and smiled.

'What is your name, child?'

'Tarana,' she said.

'This is your home now, and you will look after my girls. You will clean and help with cooking.'

'But I don't know how to cook,' Tarana said. 'I can clean and look after everyone as I did at home, but I must go to my family. They will be looking for me. And my prize at school—what'll happen to that?'

'I don't care,' the woman said. 'I have paid, ₹2000 (rupees) to the *Pradhan*, and he promised to get me an older girl.'

Tarana started crying in despair, realising she had been tricked, and she would never see her family again. After what seemed like an eternity, the woman who had opened the door came to get her. 'I'm Champa,' she said. 'Let me show you around.'

Robot-like Tarana followed Champa from room to room and ultimately reached the kitchen. A few girls were making lunch—*roti* and vegetables; they smiled and welcomed her. Everyone was a *Didi*, and the older woman was called *Amma*. 'Don't argue with *Amma*,' they warned her. 'Do your work, and she won't trouble you—she's kind.'

Tarana had no idea how the days, weeks, months, and years passed. Her tiny body was exhausted from waking up at dawn and working until midnight. The *Didis* dressed and entertained men by singing and dancing every evening, taking them to one of the many rooms.

Sometimes, the *Didis* would talk about their past lives—how they had been tricked by trusted people and dropped at *Amma's*. Some said it was their choice, as this was the only way they could support their families. Tarana realised everyone had similar stories, and there was no way out. Once she grew up, she would become like one of them.

One of Tarana's daily tasks was to get cigarettes and *paan* for *Amma*. Bilal *Bhai's* shop was five minutes away, and he gave her monthly credit. He was always kind and became her confidante, sharing her past and present life. He listened patiently and sometimes gave her a packet of biscuits, a bar of chocolate, or a lolly.

On one such visit, she noticed a man talking animatedly to Bilal Bhai. Although he looked non-descriptive something in the way he spoke touched a chord in Tarana's heart. She stood and listened to his story of losing a child and a wife who took her own life. Then, Tarana related her own story to him.

'But you're a child,' he said. 'How can anyone sell you for, ₹2000?'

'This is Musa, my cousin,' Bilal *Bhai* said. 'He lives in Meerut and is visiting.'

That was the beginning of an unusual friendship. Musa would often listen to Tarana talk about her life at *Amma's*, the family she left behind, and her aspirations and dreams. One day, he said, 'I will get you out of this place and give you a proper life. I will speak with *Amma* tomorrow.'

The following day, he was at *Amma's*. 'I want to take Tarana from here.'

'Are you going to marry her?' *Amma* laughed. 'She's a child—hasn't attained puberty yet.'

'No, I want to adopt her as my daughter.'

'You must pay me, ₹5000 for her release. I have looked after her these past 2 years,' Amma said.

'But I don't have that kind of money. I'm only a *darwan* at a school.'

Amma didn't relent. 'I will return with the money,' Musa said with an air of finality.

Tarana couldn't remember if it was months or a year before Musa returned with the money, but he bought her release from *Amma*. The sun shone brighter that day, and Tarana had an extra skip in her step. She didn't know what her future would be like, but she knew it would be better than her current life. Musa's house in the slums was smaller than *Amma's,* but Tarana felt a sense of peace and happiness that she hadn't felt in years. The people in the slum gathered around Musa and asked pointed questions about their relationship.

'You're my daughter,' Musa said. 'I will adopt you, and from today you're Tara—my brightest light.'

'What shall I call you?' Tarana asked.

'Whatever you want,' he answered.

'May I call you *Baba*?'

Tears rolled down Musa's face as his answer.

It wasn't an easy life in the slums. As a *darwan,* Baba's earnings were meagre, and he had borrowed heavily to secure her release, but they were happy. He looked after her; the one room became her refuge, a place she called home.

Tara was enrolled in *Baba's* school. Although being the eldest in her class was embarrassing—having missed years of school—Tara was determined to work hard. Once the teachers realised her potential, they encouraged her, organising coaching classes after school. Soon, she was one among equals.

'What do you want to be when you graduate school?' *Baba* asked Tara one day.

'I want to be a social worker and get a Bachelor of Social Work degree,' she said. 'No girl should go through what I did—I want to bring awareness and talk of the dangers lurking at people's doorsteps. Not everyone has a *Baba*.'

'Do you have to go to Delhi for this course?' he asked. Tara nodded.

'You must follow your passion and not worry about your tuition fees.'

'I will pitch in, *Baba*,' she said. 'You shouldn't have to carry my burden for the rest of your life.'

Soon, Tara started earning money by tutoring younger children and working at coaching centres. She kept aside some of that money for her college fees and gave the rest to *Baba*.

She moved to Delhi and stayed in a girls´ hostel for a few years, where life wasn't easy. She was relentlessly bullied both at the hostel and college. People made fun of her accent, her clothes, and her poverty, but nothing could deter her.

Two of Tara's lecturers took her under their wing after they heard her story and introduced her to social workers and the police. She accompanied them on hot and rainy days, learning the ropes. When she completed her degree, one of the social workers offered her a job in her organisation. It wasn't much, but it was a start.

Initially, she rescued two or three girls every few months, but as she became known in the sector, she worked with the police to solve more complex cases. Despite the long hours and brushes with the mafia and politicians, Tara knew this was her calling. *Baba* cheered her on from the sides, proudly sharing her achievements with everyone.

SHE *Connects*

It took her 10 years to save enough money to put a deposit for a house—a home which she hoped to share with Baba. Despite cajoling, *Baba* didn't want to leave his job and, when questioned, would say, 'What will I do if I don't work? You are not there with me anymore.'

'Come and stay with me, *Baba*,' was Tara's counterargument.

'But I don't know anyone in Delhi. This is my home and yours. You come and go as you please.'

But now, within six months, she would have a home of their own; she would no longer listen to him. For the past year, he looked a little pale and weak every time she saw him. Visits to the doctor yielded no results. This Sunday, when she would visit him, she would say enough was enough.

The call came in the early hours of the morning. Groggily, she picked up her phone and heard the news from a neighbour—news she had dreaded for months. Without a backward glance, she left for the last time to see *Baba*.

She saw the lifeless body of the man who had meant so much to her—he wasn't her blood, yet to her, he was more than any parent, any blood relative.

'Wake up, *Baba*, I'm here. I'm your Tara.' But the bony fingers didn't clutch her hands! And then the tears started.

Glossary

Baba: father.
Pradhan: village elder.
Pandaveshwar: a district in West Bengal, India.
Abba: Father.
Rickshaw: hand-held two-wheeler.
₹: symbol of the Indian rupee.
Roti: Indian flatbread.
Didi: elder sister.
Amma: mother.
Paan: betel leaf.
Bhai: elder brother.
Darwan: gatekeeper.
Birbhum: a district in West Bengal, India.

SAKHA!
O FILOS MOU!

DEBALEENA MUKHERJEE, INDIA

Characters: Draupadi, Krishna, Helen, Andromache and
'She': the author.
Place: The battlefields of Kurukshetra and Troy,
as 'She' imagines them.
Time: the past – in the epic.
The present – in her story.

The battlefields were red with dust and jet sprays of blood. The sky did not matter; the earth did not matter; only dust and death mattered. At sunrise, a *conch* made the clarion call for war at *Kurukshetra*. A horn made the clarion call on the ramparts of Troy. The two women had been blamed. Draupadi should have forgiven her humiliation, and Helen should have resisted temptation. Their harsh laughter rasped across *Ilium* and *Indraprastha* when they heard the blame, terrifying the world. Draupadi stands at her palace window, staring at her life; Helen stands on the walls of Troy, staring at hers. Both are not thoughtful. They are numb with remembrance and thrumming with the reminder—'do not forget!' Krishna comes swift-footed and stands next to Draupadi. He has access to her chambers and her thoughts, not as a God but as a friend. Silent and powerful, he waits. Friends wait quietly for as long as it takes for a friend to speak. Friendship is comfortable, versatile, and very tender. Had she not wrapped some cloth around his finger when the divine discus had nicked his skin? People look askance at them, but friends do not heed social approbation. This was not about dynasty or possessive claims—two friends being there for each other. He would have taught her to play dice if she had asked.

75

Then, on that day, she would have flung the winning dice as Krishna would have cheered. She would have realigned the fates. Draupadi trembles a little; Krishna sees her trembling. She turns to him: 'The perpetrator has been slayed, I am vindicated. I cannot be a hypocrite and say I will forget. I will not forget anyone, Krishna. Least of all …' she trails off. The *Pandavas* could be pitied and forgiven, but forget! She chooses not to forget. She looks at him and says: '*Sakha,* do you judge me for being myself?' He replies: 'No! I am with you, as I had been in that hour!' Now, Draupadi allows her pent-up sobs to tear through her body as she clings to Krishna's hands. She gasps: 'Be that friend who does not blame my beauty for people's wrong choices.' On that day, when the enemies had ripped at her garments, he had sent divine raiment to protect her modesty, and the court had cowed at this divine revelation. Draupadi's faith in her *sakha* had been steadfast.

Draupadi throws back her head and laughs. The laugh rings down the corridors of the perpetrators, and they are afraid. Modesty! She is contemptuous ... *Sakha* had not sent that cloth for her modesty: she who is born of fire. Leaping flames, never fear nudity. Flames are as naked as her wrath and as devastating as war. She had not crossed her arms across her breasts in an agony of shame. She had raised her head—her black tresses streaming with the flames of anger. They had violated her freedom of choice. They had tried to make her lose herself.

Helen watches Hector's body being dragged around that battlefield. The grief-stricken king howls: 'She is accursed!' Helen stands rigid, unmoving, her stony eyes following this savagery. She hears the winds from the Aegean Sea, tossing her golden tresses. She is beautiful and comfortable with her beauty. The Trojans call her arrogant because she does not seek their validation. It is not defiance, but she does not need forgiveness. She has loved just as much as Paris has loved. She has not lured him, neither is she 'the face that launched a thousand ships.' She stands alone and

77

chooses loneliness, not guilt. A sobbing sigh echoes in her ear. Andromache is standing beside her. Helen stiffens. Andromache gently puts her hand on Helen's head in tearful questioning.

'Helen! Hector did not have to fight today. He chose to. I had asked him to refuse Priam for the sake of our baby. He spoke of duty. He decided to prove a point rather than prove himself a parent. This war is not about you, Helen. Both of us said no to war because we believe in love. Do not blame yourself. I don't. I blame them all, but you—never. I know what you went through in Troy because you came with Paris. He was absolved; you became the seductress. You did not seduce; you loved Paris! Pay no heed. They will blame me now as the wife who did not appease the gods, but I will be condemned as weak if I wail. I will be doubly blamed, but I will not heed. I need a friend, Helen. Let us be friends. Not because we are unimportant to Troy, but because we are important to ourselves. Helen, be my friend, not in pity but as kindred spirits. Hector was my husband, never my partner.'

Helen weeps: 'Paris never knew me. I was his trophy. Yes, we will be friends, not in sympathy but in empathy. Troy burns because their egos would not back down. Andromache, you are a woman bold and thoughtful.' She gasps: 'Be that friend who does not blame my beauty for people's wrong choices.'

'Yes, Helen! A king may forbid, but we choose friendship.' Both look at that field where Hector's corpse is being dragged around in a demented frenzy. Helen looks at Andromache. She is weeping silently, her eyes fixed not on Hector's corpse but at the horizon of the Aegean Sea. She wipes her tears. Both queens wipe their tears because this war is not about them. They have been blamed and labelled. *Amazons* are labelled "mannish" because they cut off a breast to fit bows and arrows. Always a label, never the name.

II.

Place: a little study where she is writing
Time: then in the epic, now in her story

She sits, looking at the laptop screen. It reflects
the ruins of an ancient city by the sea, superimposed by
the reflection of horse riders and a solitary Krishna.
Yesterday, she read portions of *The Iliad* again and then
the middle portions of *Mahabharata*. She has to write
this little story from these ancient epics and immerse
herself in them to keep her story afloat. The epics may
be mighty, but Draupadi and Helen need the storyteller.
Now.

She continues writing: Krishna is God, and his
name is always merged with his beloved. But in this one
incarnation, he is a woman's friend—Draupadi's *sakha*, a
friend who acknowledges her femininity, respects her
sexuality, and never judges. He is her best friend. As a
friend he can praise without reservations because he
does not covet. They need only friendship. Both of

these women are not alone. They have a friend to honour their entities, not judge their reasons. A relationship is the crux. Someone hugs a tree to save it. Girls are wedded to holy rocks to save them from the perdition of widowhood, observances. Gods are wedded to feminine vegetation for the fruition of seasons. Earth herself nurtures and yields.

　　　　She pauses. In the angst of a woman alone against the world, she had forgotten her friendship bonds. This story is her epiphany that unusual relationships are not unreal. Friendship is an inclusive silence of conversations unlimited. Draupadi's fury consumed her in burning tears, and now she maintains a ferocious silence while her *Sakha* stands by her, silently and eloquently supporting her. Helen has become aloof in the face of accusations, but Andromache touches her head with a friend's blessing and support. Her fingers fly across the keyboard as she writes these words. This story is not factual, but who could say it is untrue? 'Why?' her editor would ask. 'Why this bonding? Why choose friendship and not passion as the theme?' She would reply—not as a question, but as a statement: 'Why not!' She writes: A kindred spirit says to Helen: 'You are not alone!' A kindred spirit says to Draupadi: 'You are not alone!' *Kurukshetra* and Troy have happened, Draupadi of the flames, and Helen of a thousand ships have been blamed. But it does not matter. One person has been there for them; such friendship is enough for a woman. She types swiftly: Remember the good bonds. Draupadi, Helen, Andromache, and Krishna crowd her little study, peering over her shoulder at her laptop. A teardrop from the turbulence in the thousand ships spills on the keyboard, a flame licks across her fingers, and a flute's note ripples across the screen. Yes, she has written one story with two tales. She has forged frames for friendship. A hand quietly turns on her reading light. She blinks and sees better. She types her favourite quote with an unnamed urgency, *'Kindred spirits are not so scarce as I used to think. It's splendid to find so many of them in the world.'*

82

SHE Connects

She nods at her story about kindred spirits. Then she hits the send button.

Glossary

Sakha: male friend.
O Fílos mou: Greek—my friend.
Ilium: another name for the city of Troy in the epic The Iliad.
Kurukshetra: in India, a region in the epic Mahabharata. The war between the Pandavas and the Kauravas occurred thousands of years ago.
Indraprastha: ancient India, a city ruled by the Pandavas.
Pandavas: the protagonists of Mahabharata.
Draupadi: the queen married to the five Pandavas in the Mahabharata. She was born from fire.
Krishna: eighth incarnation of Lord Vishnu.
Helen: in the Iliad, a queen of Sparta who was abducted by Paris—the prince of Troy.
Hector: Prince of Troy.
Andromache: Hector's wife.
Amazon: characters from Homer's epic The Odyssey.
'Kindred spirits …the world.': Anne of Green Gables by L.M. Montgomery.
'face that launched a thousand ships': description of Helen's beauty. A quote from Doctor Faustus by Christopher Marlowe.

THE GOLDEN EMBRACE

JESLEEN GILL PAPNEJA, USA

The taxi came to a stop outside the gates of Belvedere Palace. Rubina looked up at the palace, the tears she had been forcing back were threatening to shake loose again. It had been months since Kian's death. Whereas her world had come to a screeching halt, the world outside seemed to have moved on with cruel indifference. His sudden, tragic accident had shattered her in a way she hadn't anticipated. Every day since, it had felt like wading through a thick fog, where even the most basic acts of living seemed to take tremendous effort. Rubina felt lost, stranded in the wreckage of her grief.

Their life together had always been filled with vibrant colours—mainly reflected in her paintings. Their shared laughter would echo long into the night. But now, the colours had drained away, leaving her in a world of grey. She couldn't find joy in anything, not even in her art. Rubina, once an aspiring painter, hadn't picked up a brush since Kian's passing. She would wake up each day, get ready and go to work like a wooden soldier. She would spend the day at her art gallery meeting people without mentally acknowledging their presence and answering their questions mechanically, falling back on her muscle memory. At home, in the evenings, she watched videos and photos of Kian and herself as she sipped wine, often falling asleep with her laptop on and the empty wine bottle rolling around on the floor. The next day would be a repeat of the previous.

SHE Connects

One Saturday afternoon, in desperation, she found herself wandering the city streets, seeking something—anything—that might bring her some relief. Her feet carried her to Belvedere Palace, a gallery where she and Kian had spent countless afternoons, lost in the works of great artists. She didn't know why she'd come. The idea of being surrounded by art, which had once been a passion she shared with Kian, now felt like a cruel reminder of what she had lost. She stood across the street as though paralysed, but she couldn't bring herself to go in. The busy street before the palace almost ceased as Rubina fell into a trance. She was jolted out of it by a bus's rude, loud horn. As she looked up at the noise source, he realised that she had unknowingly walked into the middle of the street and was holding up traffic. She moved quickly and crossed over to the side of the street where the palace stood. She found the visitor centre, bought her ticket and entered the palace courtyard.

Rubina stood in the courtyard and inhaled deeply. It was as though the air had imbibed his cologne and was gently mixing it with the fragrance of the flowers. The fountain where they clicked countless selfies was still there. The blue sky and the clouds seemed to remember their configuration and appeared, smiling down at her. Once inside the gallery, she wandered, her eyes gliding over the paintings. Then suddenly, she turned a corner and stopped dead in her tracks. There it was—*The Kiss* by Gustav Klimt.

Kian and she had always admired Klimt's work. His lavish use of gold, his swirling patterns, and the way he captured intimacy and sensuality had always spoken to her. But now, standing in front of *The Kiss*, she felt something stir deep within her.

The painting depicted a man and a woman wrapped in a golden embrace, their bodies entwined in a sea of shimmering gold. Their faces were close, and their lips were on the verge of meeting. The man's hands gently cradled the woman's face as if he held his entire world. The woman, eyes closed, seemed to melt into the embrace, her expression serene, trusting, and utterly at peace.

Rubina stood there, transfixed, tears welling up in her eyes. The longer she looked at the painting, the more she felt an unexpected sensation rising in her chest—a sense of comfort.

For the first time since Kian's death, Rubina allowed herself to truly feel the full weight of her grief. She let the tears flow freely, unashamed, indifferent to the strangers who walked by. There, amid the gallery, she sobbed. But it wasn't the kind of helpless sobbing she had done so many times. This was different. There was a release in it, a letting go that she hadn't felt before.

It was as though Klimt's golden embrace was speaking directly to her with all its warmth and tenderness. It wasn't the man's arms around the woman that mattered—it was the woman's surrender, the letting go. The woman in the painting wasn't holding on; she was allowing herself to be held. She was surrendering, not to the man, but to the moment, the love, and something more significant than herself. And at that moment came Rubina's epiphany – that love, even in the face of death, doesn't end. The love she shared with Kian will always be with her, just as the golden light in *The Kiss* seemed to shine beyond the figures themselves. It is eternal, not in a way that ties her down, but in a way that sets her free.

For months, Rubina had been fighting against the tide of her grief, trying to control it, suppress it, or push it away. She had tried to hold on to Kian and the life they were supposed to have. But here, before Klimt's masterpiece, she realised she didn't need to hold on any more. She could let go, not of her love for Kian, but of the pain wrapped around it like a shroud. Rubina stood there for what felt like hours, letting the painting wash over her, its golden light enveloping her like the warmth of a long-lost embrace. She understood now. She didn't need to forget Kian to move on. She could carry him with her, like the woman in the painting— held, cherished, but free. She didn't need to control her grief or banish it. She could simply let it be and, in doing so, find peace.

The following day, Rubina did something she hadn't done in months: she picked up her paintbrush. At first, her hand trembled, unsure of itself, but soon, the brush moved smoothly across the canvas. She painted without thinking, letting the colours flow, and her emotions guide her. By the time she stepped back, her heartfelt lighter. On the canvas was an abstract swirl of gold, reds, and greens, a homage to Klimt's work but uniquely hers. It wasn't the painting that mattered—it was the act. For the first time in months, Rubina had created something. She had taken a step forward. The colours returned to her life slowly and subtly, but they were there.

Rubina smiled softly to herself. Kian's memory would always be a part of her, but now, she could begin to let go of the pain and hold on to the love. Just like the golden figures in Klimt's *The Kiss*, she could surrender to the moment, to life, and trust that she would be held, cherished, and at peace.

Having that unexpected epiphany, Rubina secured her relationship with *The Kiss* and finally found her reprieve in that improbable place.

Epilogue

My story, The Golden Embrace, is not just about Rubina's journey of coming to terms with Kian's death; it is a deeper exploration of what it means to lead a peaceful and fulfilling life. Through Rubina's connection with Klimt's The Kiss, I seek to capture the emotional and symbolic essence of surrendering control and embracing the art of letting go.

As humans, we often tend to cling tightly to people, situations, and outcomes, inadvertently creating stress and suffering. But like Rubina, when we allow ourselves to be held—rather than relentlessly holding on—we open the door to profound peace and freedom. This shift in perspective is not just a moment of growth but a transformative human epiphany, one that resonates deeply with the universal quest for serenity and self-discovery.

91

THE

MESSENGER

ABHILASHA KUMAR, SWITZERLAND

Dear Universe,

I haven't written you one of these letters in a long time. I had lost faith in my ability to decode your metaphysical messages and cosmic whispers. There had been too much misjudgment on my part.

At what point did you decide to rescue me? Was it that day in the kitchen when the dam within finally burst, and I wept over the thousand glass pieces flung far and wide on the kitchen floor, much like the pieces of my life? That was the glass jar from my wedding. Just a wispy memory by then. Or was it that night when I stared at the full moon from the balcony and screamed silently, why am I here? Just tell me! Or was it when the blinking cursor stood still on the blank Word page like a ticking clock counting eternity?

Soon thereafter, change arrived so smoothly. Like one's inhalation and exhalation. First, it was the invitation to join the work meeting in South Africa. Then, my colleagues and I decided to extend the work trip to visit Kruger Park. It led to that chance meeting with the South African couple during breakfast on the last day in Kruger. We had a day's time on our hands, and the lady suggested visiting the numerous stone circles in the Mpumalanga area. I cannot recall how the conversation led her to mention Adam's Calendar. But when she did, a mild electric current ran up my spine like a dead battery had sputtered to life.

I can still recall the joy I felt when our caravan approached the quaint village of Kaapschehoop, just two miles from Adam's Calendar. If that lady had not insisted that we go there first because we would not understand the stones without a proper guide, your cosmic plot could not have reached fruition. Kaapschehoop was a beautiful Nordic-style village nestled amid the panoramic Mpumalanga mountains. It was picture-perfect, but was as dead as a provincial French town at night. Not a soul was in sight, save the large Bavarian lady at the German café. She knew two guides.

We had no way of knowing then that both phone numbers that she had given us turned out to be a couple sitting side by side at a barbecue picnic with friends that Sunday afternoon. I called Sam first. Sam, with his deep voice and thick South African accent, declined the request to take me on the tour. Then, I called Rachel. 'Wait a minute! Didn't you just call Sam?' she asked with amusement. 'Yes, but how do you know?' I asked her stupidly. 'Because he is my partner and is sitting next to me,' she laughed, returning the phone to Sam.

'I can take you there tomorrow. I don't work on Sundays,' he said.

'But my flight out of South Africa is tomorrow morning,' I protested.

You were testing me. The more it seemed that the opportunity was slipping away, the more determined I felt to visit Adam's Calendar. Something tenacious and ancient was beckoning me.

Then, as if to test my resolve, Sam called me back after a few minutes. 'Usually, it costs 150 rands. But as you are so obviously desperate to go there, I can tear myself away from this beautiful Sunday afternoon for 400 rands,' he said. He knew it was an exorbitant sum!

Everyone else refused to go at that point—everyone except me. I needed to go. There was no rational reason. It was just a pull I couldn't explain, like a nail may feel for the magnet. Sam was a far cry from the urban men I was used to. I thought he was uppity when he said on the phone, 'Bring along warm clothes, sturdy shoes and a good attitude.' Then I met him. I can still picture that worn-out pickup truck rolling into the main village street. When he stepped out, he looked like a cross between a wild cowboy, a Native American Indian, and a farmer. He was the spitting image of the Hollywood actor Donald Sutherland. Only Sam was taller and stouter, with a hint of beer belly peeping through his jacket. Salt and pepper hair in need of a haircut framed his face. He wore beaded bracelets on both wrists. An eagle's talon hung around his neck. Wrinkles spread around his blue eyes, like ripples on a still lake.

The sight of him didn't make my heart leap at all. Yet, something about him warmed the heart, like the sun gradually cutting through an icy glacier. His sudden, unexpected embrace made me blush. I wasn't used to strangers greeting me in that manner.

SHE *Connects*

As I entered the pickup truck, I noticed a collection of axes, knives, sickles, and hammers casually lying under the passenger seat. Was he a tour guide, a farmer or a serial killer? A big ice cooler sat between the passenger and driver's seats. 'Drinks from the picnic,' he replied casually, following my glance. The car's leather seats were torn and mottled, with foam peeping out. That vehicle had not seen a garage since its manufacturing days.

We set off towards the stone ruins, winding down circuitous roads. Winter's chill caressed my face. We reached Adam's Calendar with just two and a half hours of daylight left. A meaningless rusty gate with a chained padlock stood in the middle of green pastures, as if to discourage visitors. A rickety, vestigial sign saying 'Blue Swallow Sanctuary' was next to the gate. Sam informed me that the migratory blue swallows had stopped coming there for years and, sadly, were on the brink of extinction.

Wild horses grazed around the dolerite stone ruins. They were the only visible beings for miles.

Sam offered me a beer from the ice cooler. I didn't drink beer. 'Oh, I am so sorry for you,' he shrugged, opening a bottle for himself. 'Wine then? Water?'

'No, thanks; I am alright,' I said awkwardly. I had to avert my eyes from his intense gaze.

I took in the magnificence before me. The pastures led to a steep cliff with a breathtaking 200-meter drop into the valley below.

Unexpectedly, Sam said, 'I don't know why I am meant to meet you for just two hours in my life.' He shook his head, ran his hands through his hair, and declared that he was very happy and excited to meet me. As we stood looking at each other, an unfamiliar telepathy coursed through us – a mutual exchange of wordless thoughts. I could hear him tell himself, 'Stop staring at her. Stop freaking her out. You are scaring her.' Having grown up in Mumbai, my instincts were razor-sharp. This was the sort of situation–desolate place with a seemingly eager stranger–that I would never get myself into. That day, however, no alarm bells were triggered. Instead, a calm intuition told me that there was no danger.

Sam showed me the lay line of the Earth that ran through the stone site. He invited me to walk on it, declaring matter-of-factly that I had walked there before. No grass grew on that magnetic line, that central *nadi* that runs through Mother Earth. A steady, palpable energy flowed through her, and, as if by extension, through my body, making its way up my spine, across my shoulders, and all the way to my fingertips. Like a mild electric current.

A distant memory stirred. I wanted to touch it, but the memory seemed to be just out of reach.

When Sam held my hand, I could not help but register the strangeness of that gesture. Yet again, no alarm bells rang. It did not feel romantic but comfortable, like an easy friendship between lifelong friends who had met after a long time.

Now, I think that he may have held my hand to connect deeper to my thoughts. Because, when we reached the main stone circle, he informed me that he was also a shaman. He had known that someone of my description would visit him towards the end of winter that year.

I do not even have a photograph of him or that magical place. I had taken out my phone to open the compass app, as Sam explained that there were abnormal magnetic currents at that site. The compass was indeed acting berserk and swung like a pendulum. My phone's battery was still half-full. Nevertheless, it died soon after, as if a fuse had blown. His phone died too. The sun sank into the horizon, inking the sky with a mélange of red and orange. It didn't take long for darkness to cast its starry blanket upon the vastness before us. The stones were still warm from the sun. I hugged them and felt their warmth seep into my chilled bones. Sam led me to the cliff's edge, next to the oldest stones. I was informed that we were standing on roughly the same longitude as the pyramids of Giza in Egypt and Mount Kailash in Tibet. Adam's Calendar was much older. Some claimed it was 75,000 years old.

Suddenly, several dogs started barking in the distance. Sam let out a loud, shrill whistle, and they fell silent at once. He smiled at me and said, 'They are my dogs. Maybe they sensed me.' They were at least a few kilometres away. I had so many questions about this eccentric man.

'Is your house in that direction?' I asked, curious. 'Yes, I moved away when Kaapschehoop became crowded. Two hundred people! That is too much for me. You don't see any lights because I live without electricity. You should try candlelight.'

I didn't know anyone who lived without electricity in this century. I did not think to ask if he had a refrigerator, how he charged his phone, or how he ploughed his fields.

I worried my colleagues would send out a search party if I didn't return soon, but Sam was determined to take his time. He sat down beside me on the warm dolerite stone by the cliff's edge; the spectacular Milky Way was directly above us.

Reading my thoughts, he continued, 'Humans almost always want to be some place other than where they are, whether it be a place or circumstance. Right now, I don't want to be anywhere else except here. We won't have this time together for a long, long time to come.'

I retorted, 'I guess it is hard to surrender to situations that present themselves. It is a futile tragedy that humans exhaust themselves fighting their fate.'

Sam picked out a word I had mentioned. 'Surrender! What is surrender, and why is it so hard?' He paused, then asked, 'Did you see any cute little lion cubs at Kruger?'

'Yes, we saw a pride with newborns.'

'Did you see how the mother holds her baby in her mouth? Sometimes, she brings it to safety. Sometimes, it is a chastisement. Did you see how the cub just lets her do it? It does not resist at all. The cub is not wondering if mother's teeth will hurt, or what if she drops it, or what if danger is around the corner. The cub just lets itself be taken wherever its mother wants. It has complete trust. This is true surrender. Trust the process. Don't resist where life takes you.'

I let his words sink in.

Then, he surprised me by asking, 'Why don't you write anymore? You can't deny yourself who you are.'

I decided not to ask him how he knew. 'It's like words are stuck inside me,' I told him candidly, 'I can't seem to lay the egg.'

He laughed heartily through his belly. 'Lay the egg! Ha!'

'Yeah, something within runs dry even before I start. Maybe I don't know what good it will do. I fear that I will just find a novel way to talk about that same old existential angst. I work in a publishing house. I have read it all: good books, bad books, terrible poetry. The good books just say it better. They just weave words more cleverly and flirt more courageously with language. But they aren't saying anything new that's not been said before. Anyway, nobody cares about what is being said. Everyone seems to care about how it's said.'

'Are you afraid nobody will care for your work?' he asked. 'No. I am just afraid I will have nothing new to say. It feels pointless.'

'Maybe you have a new way of saying the same thing? Maybe your perspective is unique and pertinent for this day and age. Maybe those who described existentialism before are archaic now. Maybe you are needed. Maybe your opinion counts. Maybe someone reads what you write, and a light switches on in their head, makes them wonder, question something, or gives them an idea. How would you know unless you tried? Maybe then, you would stop feeling so constipated.' He was so amused at the use of that expression.

You, dear universe, could not have sent me a message which was clearer than that.

'So, you are saying I should just start writing again?' I asked him.

'I am just saying that you should put your pen to paper and let the universe do its work through you,' he smiled at me then. We could not delay our return any longer. Just before we stepped inside his pickup truck, Sam declared, 'I am going to take a piss,' and headed towards the front end of the car. He bellowed, 'Gentlemen this way; ladies that way,' pointing towards the car's rear end. I did not dare to squat, even though no human was in sight. Then, most peculiarly, he said, 'All other beings, you are now free to go whichever way you want.'

We drove back to the meeting point with my colleagues, talking on the way back. Sam wanted to know everything about my life. He kept asking me questions. To my taciturn answers, he kept urging, 'Tell me more.' When I told him about the separation with Avinash, he covered my hand with his and said, 'It's nobody's fault. Sometimes, it is wiser to quit than keep trying in a relationship well past its expiry date.'

We said goodbye at the caravan. Sam didn't take a single penny for the tour. Said he couldn't. Instead, he lifted me off the ground and squeeze-hugged me so tight that my breath left my body. My colleagues looked puzzled and even suspicious. His parting words were, 'Goodbye, my soul friend. We will meet again. In another life.'

'Thank you for everything,' I said in earnest. Winking at me, he replied, 'I am only the messenger.'

Sam did mean to say goodbye for this lifetime, for he blocked my number from his phone the next day. I could not even send him a parting message. Not that it was ever needed.

Today, two years later, the rivers within, that had run dry, have swelled again. The energy that had coursed through my spine at Adam's Calendar has replenished my exhausted batteries with a new will for life. Perhaps the energy ensured that the egg was laid, and that a blinking cursor kept travelling across pages. Perhaps the messenger you sent my way also had something to do with it. Last week, *National Geographic* published an article about blue swallows starting to arrive in South Africa again, with a stronghold in the Mpumalanga area.

I am learning, dear universe, to be that little cub who surrenders to your uncanny ways.

In gratitude,

Karuna.

Glossary

Nadi: In yogic terminology, it is a psychic (subtle) channel through which energy flows.

Shaman: A practitioner who interacts with the spirit world and other realms to bring about healing for others. Typically, shamanism is practised in the North and South American, Nordic and North Asian/Siberian cultures.

ROBIDADU

KANCHANA SINGHA BOSEROY, USA

"O my sweetheart, I want you, I need you
O my bosom friend, help me, help me
O my dearest, take me to my success
With thy sweet and loving hand."

Shona opened the folded inland letter. Her fiancé had given her the letter that morning. She must have read it for the umpteenth time by now. Carefully, with reverence, she opened the letter yet again. Shona read the words, ironing out the creases, almost caressing the phrase with her gaze.

The letter, written to her fiancé by his mother Komola, came as a delightful surprise after months of prior disapproval. It was an acceptance of their relationship, a blessing. He had delivered it to Shona earlier with a big grin, as his eyes lit up with joy.

'Look, Shona,' he said with exuberance. 'Look what my mother wrote,' pointing out the paragraph in English.

Shona looked at it and began to read. The words sounded as if he, her fiancé, was talking to her directly and declaring his love to her. A promise. A plea. A proposal.

But, the words were old-fashioned. The style of writing was not his. Besides, the letter was from his mother to him.

The handwriting was his mother's. Shona recognised the English writing from the address that was always meticulously written on every inland letter he received. That was the only English she ever wrote. The rest was in Bengali, the language his mother was well versed in. She described how Shona's parents had gone to their house, and together, they agreed to the relationship, which still did not have parental approval.

This letter was to express acceptance and give blessings. Komola ended the letter with these four lines of poetry in quotation marks, written in flawless English!

Shona reread the words. This time aloud, with expression. She was trying to solve a mystery. How could Komola have written this? Granted, Komola had a flair for writing and was an avid reader. Shona had read the poetry Komola had written. She shared her literary pursuits with Shona. This was their common bond. But they were all in Bengali. Komola did not know English well and did not write poetry or even read books in English. Shona remembered that Komola had read Rebecca, written by Daphne Du Maurier and translated the book into Bengali. Shona often tried encouraging her to read in English, and she replied that it was too laborious.

'How could she possibly have written this?' Shona was bewildered.

'She didn't,' her fiancé calmly replied.

'Oh, so you did? Before? And she had it?' Shona continued to try to make sense of this.

'No, I did not,' he said. 'This is the first time I am reading this too.'

'Then, who wrote it?' Shona was totally at a loss.

'Robidadu did,' he declared.

'Robidadu? Rabindranath Tagore? The famous Nobel Laureate? The Bengali poet, philosopher, and songwriter? That Robidadu?' Shona asked, almost with sarcasm.

'But this is not published anywhere; his works in English are limited,' Shona said incredulously. Not that she was an expert. But this was not his well-known popular work. Anyway, Komola did not read English poetry. So, how could she have known this piece?

'Oh,' he clarified, 'I did not mean his already published works. I meant that these are his words through my mother's writing.'

Shona shook her head in utter disbelief. Tagore had died in 1941, and this was the 1980s. What on earth

112

did he mean? Even though he tried to explain, she did not understand what he meant then.

Months passed. Shona got married and became a welcome addition to Komola's family. Her already good relationship grew further, and she became an integral part of Komola's life—especially her intellectual, literary, and spiritual life. She was also drawn into Komola's ethereal and extraordinary clairvoyant life, as a confidante. This life connected Komola in some unknown way to the other world; a part of her life that was privy to very few.

Shona learned that Komola was different from a young age. While others were learning the domestic duties needed for the inevitable marriage market, Komola liked reading and writing. She liked the supernatural. She liked the extraordinary. Like every other Bengali, she voraciously read Tagore. But she did more. She immersed herself in him. She connected with him. She talked to him—at first, in her imagination, then through her poetry and writing. Using her unique and

113

unbelievable gift, Komola found she could communicate with him!

Shona watched this incredible event many times, after her marriage. A close loved one would hold Komola's hand, and after a period of intense longing and yearning in the minds of all present, her hand would rise automatically; then it would write in the air or fall on the tiled floor and write on it, or on paper or whatever was available. Komola would close her eyes, while sitting up straight on the floor in a trance-like state. As Shona witnessed this repeatedly, she saw how Komola's handwriting would be hers, but the words and content were not. The old-fashioned manner of speech, the use of old-world English phrases and words sometimes like "bosom friend" and "thy" were not hers. Sometimes, the writing was about events that Komola had no prior knowledge of. Sometimes, it would be answers to questions asked, and other times, it would be advice. Sometimes it would be a few lines of poetry, sometimes some prose. Sometimes it was deeply philosophical, sometimes it would be light humour. Sometimes the words were dark and foreboding, and sometimes they were a blessing.

Initially, Shona questioned this. She was sceptical. She could not understand or believe it. This was an unbelievable phenomenon that she was witnessing personally. How was this possible? Was she a medium? Was this a form of planchette? Was she connecting with a spirit? Was she a different kind of person?

She was stunned. She was in shock!

And scared. Afraid.

Slowly, she stopped rationalising. She stopped doubting. She stopped being apprehensive. She let herself be at peace. She let herself accept Komola as she was—a regular woman, a mother, a mother-in-law, a wife, a daughter, a *Boudi*—a loving person with many relationships. Yes, many relationships including a very special one with a very special person who happened to be in another world—Robidadu.

Komola continued her daily life and shared her gift with a select few. She never used or abused it but held it close to her heart. Her relationship with Robidadu was personal, ethereal, unusual, and dear to her. During times of great importance in her life, she received blessings from Robidadu, which she passed on to others. This letter was one such blessing. Those four lines were a gift from Robidadu to his dear Komola. They were a blessing for her son and his loving Shona, who would later, as prophesied by Robidadu, guide him to success with her sweet and loving hand.

Glossary

Robidadu: Dadu means maternal grandfather. Robi is short for Rabindranath (spelt phonetically). Robidadu is commonly used as an endearment for Rabindranath Tagore, a famous poet Bengalis hold dear to their hearts.

Boudi: Sister-in-law, commonly used for an elder brother's wife.

AAHELI

SREYOSHI GUHA, INDIA

I had always been Ma's shadow, her constant companion through the highs and lows of her life. My name is Aaheli, and though I cannot speak, I've always understood the unspoken words of love, sorrow, and hope that passed between us.

The monsoon rains hammered against the windows, a relentless curtain of water that blurred the outside world. The once-vibrant garden outside was a blur of dark greens and greys, the rain turning everything into a smudged watercolour painting. The house felt colder and darker, as if it were retreating into itself. Inside, Ma sat in her favourite armchair, her frail frame wrapped in a knitted shawl. Though faded, the shawl was a testament to the many years of comfort it had provided. Strong and capable, her hands trembled as she stroked my fur. I could feel her sadness in her deep sighs, her breath heavy with unspoken thoughts.

'Aaheli,' Ma said softly, her voice cracking. 'Sometimes, I wonder if I've failed. The children ... they don't seem to care anymore. Every time I call, it's either, 'Ma, why do you bother me at work?' or 'Ma, what did you do with the money I sent?'

I lifted my head, looked up at her, and tried to tell her I understood with my eyes. I nudged her hand gently, trying to offer comfort in the only way I knew. My silence was filled with empathy, my presence a small balm for her troubled heart.

'I remember when Bapi was here,' she continued, her eyes misting with memories. 'He was so happy about this house. We had so many plans ... mornings on the terrace sipping tea, outings with the granddaughters ... But then he fell ill, and just like that, he was gone. I felt the same silence then, the same emptiness.'

118

I rested my head on her lap, closing my eyes as I listened. The sound of the rain and the distant rumble of thunder filled the room, fittingly sound tracking her grief. Occasionally, lightning illuminated the room, casting eerie shadows that danced on the walls.

'*Bapi* worked so hard for *Bhai*,' Ma said, her voice trembling. 'I wish *Didi* would understand how difficult it was to support *Bhai* through his studies abroad. We had so little, even though *Bapi* was a Chartered Accountant from England. I wish she knew how tough it was to live on the little *Bhai* sent. But she never listened. She only calls when it's convenient for her.' I licked her hand, trying to offer some solace. Her tears fell silently, and I could feel the heaviness of her sorrow. I wanted to tell her that I understood that I was here for her, even if I could not express it in words.

The days grew harder for Ma. Her movements became slower, each step a painful reminder of her arthritis. The doctors had been clear: bone degeneration was taking its toll, and there was nothing more to be done. 'When is Ma coming back?' I heard *Bhai's* voice, full of frustration, as he spoke over the phone to Madan *da*, her helper. They said they were taking her to the hospital. Why is there an ominous silence'?

I moved slowly through the house, each step a struggle. The once-vibrant home was now filled with an oppressive quiet. The old wooden stairs creaked under my weight, each sound a ghost of the lively days we once knew. I remembered the day we first moved in. *Bapi* had been so excited, so hopeful for the future. His dreams had been filled with laughter and the clinking of tea cups on the terrace, but fate had taken him too soon. The memories of his enthusiasm for the house and his dreams for the granddaughters lingered in the empty spaces.

'Ma, why do you keep calling me when I'm at work?' *Bhai's* harsh words echoed in my mind. 'Do you need money again? What did you do with the 1 *lac* I sent six months ago? How could you spend it so fast?'

I could feel Ma's heartbreak as she cried, her body trembling with silent sobs. I wished I could speak and tell *Bhai* how hard it was for Ma to manage the little he sent and how much Bapi had sacrificed to support him. But Ma remained silent, her tears the only testament to her suffering. I stayed by her side, my presence a small comfort.

ßThe doorbell's sound cut through the silence. I wished I could have leapt up and rushed to answer it, but my arthritis kept me from moving quickly. I made my way slowly to the door, hoping against hope that it was Ma returning from the hospital. When *Mashi* opened the door, *Didi* stood there, her face streaked with tears. 'Ma, why couldn't you have waited a few more hours?' she cried, her voice breaking. 'I was coming by the first flight. Maybe I could have taken you to a better hospital. Did someone poison you for your property? I didn't even get a chance to say sorry, to tell you I loved you.' Her grief was palpable, and I watched helplessly as she wept. I vividly remember the day Didi came for an unexpected visit from Delhi. Her shock and anger had been apparent when she found Ma's helpers in the room.

'Ma, how could you do this?' Didi had screamed. 'Why is your driver's family in your room? The maid's father sitting on your bed and holding your hand? How could you do this?'

That was five years ago. Didi had not visited since. She would never know the loneliness Ma had endured, the fear of dwindling resources, and the mounting medical bills. Ma had clung to her helpers, who had become her only source of comfort. To the world, it seemed unusual, but to Ma, they were her companions in her final years.

As I lay by Ma's side, I remember having watched Ma's final moments unfold with a heavy heart. The rain had stopped, leaving in its wake a heavy oppressive silence. Her breathing had grown shallower and her once bright eyes dim. 'I wish ...' she whispered, her voice barely audible. 'I wish I could have seen you all one last time and told you everything that was in my heart. But now, it's too late.'

Her gaze fell on me, lying beside her. Her hand reached out, weakly stroking my fur. "Thank you, Aaheli, for being with me," she murmured, her voice a fragile whisper.

I remained by her side, my presence a silent testament to our bond. Her eyes slowly closed, and her breathing grew fainter. The room was still, and the silence was profound.

As I watched Ma's final moments, I felt a deep sadness. I was the last witness to her life, her loyal companion in her final days. When Ma's breathing finally ceased, the house fell into an even more profound silence. The air seemed to hold its breath, mourning her passing. I stayed by her side, my heart heavy with the weight of our shared memories. I lifted my head and howled, letting my anguish seep into the atmosphere. Later, as the house was filled with mourning, I knew I would remain a silent witness to the end of her story. Ma had left behind a world filled with unspoken words and unresolved pain, and I, Aaheli, would carry her memory in my heart forever. The rain had begun again, a gentle patter against the windows, as if the heavens were shedding tears for her passing. And I, alone but resolute, would honour her memory in the quiet company of our home.

Glossary

Aaheli: Pure.
Ma: mother.
Bapi: father.
Didi: sister.
Bhai: Brother.

TICK TOCK

RITI GANGOPADHYAY-MUKHERJEE,

SWITZERLAND

It was rather bulky.

Chipped off at one side, just like my front teeth. It had been given to me by my father. It was mine—the only thing that solely belonged to me. Ma made sure everything was packed out of the house along with me. My childhood toys, books, family presents, and my grandfather's clock—the one my father gave me. There were also brand-new sarees and ornaments for my husband's family members. Of course, for me, too—shoes and blouses that matched each saree, ornaments, and bags that boasted traditional marriage. But somehow, I felt all of me and my

125

childhood left that morning. Ma, clad in her white cotton saree, barefoot, stood pale as the taxi started. She shoved the keys of the clock into my hands and seemed to say something to it.

I thought I heard 'Be with her' but was unsure. She whispered something as she caressed me and the clock and said goodbye. It was half past five in the morning, and the red vermillion ceremony was going to be held at my husband's house 150 kilometres from Calcutta.

None of them spoke to me, the innate abjects that silently carried lots of laughter and memories, except one that loyally stayed alive to accompany me to my new house—the wall clock. It ticked constantly throughout the journey from the city to the outskirts of Calcutta.

Ma had given me the clock's keys, and I held them gently. The key was the clock's lifeline and perhaps the only thing for me that connected me to the home I had grown up in. It was also the key to my memories and dreams I was leaving behind its shut doors.

Life at my husband's house was different from my earlier life. I had to stand in line with two plastic buckets to get water, as none was available after 9 a.m. This was something I was not used to. My mind wandered into my home bathroom, which had clean running water flowing through the taps. My heart beat loudly every time I stood in line, and the only other beat that ever understood my feelings was the ticking of the clock. It loosely stood at the corner of my room, on the terrace.

My life with my husband was indifferent, and he barely spoke with me. He was a graduate, while I had just completed higher secondary school. My college was learning life hands-on!

While my husband travelled to Kolkata for work, I watched TV every morning after finishing my work. I loved seeing women walk the ramp in clothes that shaped their bodies and shampoos that turned their hair silken, women who read the news, and women who romanced their husbands, sometimes men who were not their husbands. These thoughts thrilled me.

I was beautiful too, and after my shower, when the red cotton towel cloth hugged my body, it looked just as shapely as the woman on the black and white screen. I smiled shyly every time I felt a current pass through my body. I looked at the clock ticking at the corner—my friend from childhood. It seemed to know every little thought that passed through my mind. I covered its round face with another saree lest it saw me bare while I dried myself and changed into my daily wear, after which I winked shyly at it and patted its head as I left the terrace room to go into the kitchen to cook for the family. Alas, its hands were too short to hold me!

The afternoon was ours, too. I would lie close to the clock, and its ticking gave me a warmth that I cannot explain—a touch that caressed me without tou-ching; the sound looked through me as my best friend would, and its tick-tock matched the rhythm of my heartbeat. I loved the frisson of electric current running through my whole body most afternoons—a current I wanted to feel when my husband held me—but never did. His was a cold, wild grasp. But this feeling was different—it made me close my eyes and want to sit beside my childhood friend—closer and closer and put my head on the wooden head of the clock that ticked-tocked without fail. All for me! We started living together for each other. I had four children through the cold, wild grasps, and they grew up listening to the steady rhythmic beats of my childhood friend who never let us down. I wound it religiously every week, and it lived and loved me.

We both beat at our rhythms without fail. I cried and laughed with it. I drew to give it a face, limbs, and a heart!

We both aged. My coconut-oiled hair grew thinner and grey before turning white and falling off. My skin was wrinkled, and the veins stood out against the pale, dry skin. My friend grew older, too. The hardwood lost its shine, the gold from its numbers faded, and the silver hands looked worn out. We were both running out of time.

I could hardly move anymore. I dragged myself closer to my friend, and our hearts beat silently through the hot afternoons. My children kept water for me at my bedside and old sarees with which I wiped the blood from every cough.

We were both trying hard to be alive.

We both remembered the day we left home, and I knew that as long as the clock ticked, my heart would, too. I gathered all my strength to wind it every day at dusk before we slept through the night.

I hardly saw the father of my children. He lived in Kolkata. Rumours had it that he had remarried and had another family. Funnily, I wasn't hurt.

That day, I only had the strength to wind my companion for years halfway, and that too at intervals. The cough was endless, and so was the blood. The village doctor gave his word and left. I looked into my friend's eyes, who had never left my side. I clutched the keys my mother had given me with my left hand and tried to touch it with my right. We were fighting to breathe; our hearts ticked together for a couple of hours, and suddenly, there was silence. It was half past five in the afternoon.

I remember someone saying, 'This is good wood. We can use it as a part of the pyre.' I imagined myself on it, wrapped together in white, our bodies touching, and although none of us had a heartbeat anymore, we were together. I imagined us both being lit by the burning sandalwood twig that would turn us into ashes, where we would be soot together. No one could tell which part of the soot was me and which part was my ticking friend's.

THE GIRL AND THE TORTOISE

SONIA KULLAR, INDIA

'Mom! Look at what the Wicked Lady gave us!' Smita burst into the house carrying an enamel basin filled with sand. Scrambling around in it was a small tortoise, the size of a teacup.

Mom finally understood what the children were saying. The tall, purple-haired lady with an imperious air, whom they had dubbed Wicked Lady, had given them her grandson's pet since he had returned to England.

'Let's call him Mr. Plod,' suggested Mira, the wise elder sister. 'Yes, like the policeman in Noddy's books,' Samit nodded.

Mom placed it in the empty aquarium. Smita would talk to him every day. He seemed to recognise her voice, appearing from among the rocks and driftwood he loved to hide behind when she called out.

She would watch him in amusement as he marched up and down, up and down the aquarium. Or pushed sand into his drinking water.

'Look, Mom,' she exclaimed one day. 'He's following me!' He would walk in tandem with her as she walked alongside his aquarium.

Smita was a cute dumpling of a child with dimpled cheeks, large eyes and an innocent, loving demeanour.

The youngest among her siblings, she was the darling of the family. However, she was often left to her own devices, especially as the others needed to focus on schoolwork.

Mr. Plod became her solace. She would talk to him, share her day, and show him her drawings. She began sharing what he 'said' back to her. He was her confidante and playmate.

Years passed. Mira and Samit relocated to college. Mr. Plod, in the meanwhile, had begun showing interesting streaks in his character. For one, he had grown almost as large as a saucer. When Smita spoke, he'd poke his head out, turning towards her voice. For anyone else, he quickly ducked into his shell. The aquarium broke, and he was back in a basin. He learned to scramble out of it very quickly. This became a game between Smita and him. She'd plonk him in the basin, telling him to be a good boy, and within a few minutes, he would be out. He had become adventurous, exploring the house, and was often found under the bed in the adjoining room.

One day, Smita giggled, 'Mom, look, he's walking towards the kitchen. He's hungry!'

He cheered her up as no one else could. Sad and lonely after her siblings had moved out to different cities, he brought laughter into her life. Often unwilling to leave her bed, Mr. Plod and his shenanigans would make her smile. She poured her heart out to him, and he seemed to listen carefully, feet and head splayed out of his shell.

'I miss Mira and Samit, Plod. They used to tease me, but we'd play so much. Now, I've been left behind.'

She shared her aspirations with him—to be a musician and a teacher, to be 'cool' and go to parties. He was her sole companion very often. There was no internet and no easy access to phones. Long-distance calls had to be planned and booked and were cut off after 3 minutes. Her mother tried to take her to libraries to invite other children home, but she still spent long hours alone.

Mr. Plod snoozed at Smita's feet, often as she plucked the chords of her guitar. He followed her around the house, moving quite quickly. When he heard a different tread or the swish of Mom's sari, he'd stop short and disappear into his shell as though to say, 'Who, me? I'm not here. I'm asleep in my shell.'

His tastes had now widened. No longer did he want limp, tasteless lettuce. He loved the peels of almost every vegetable and ate them with glee. He arrived in the kitchen well in time for his meal, pulling at the maid's sari as she sat on her haunches to cut and chop till she set out his little plate for him. She would break into peals of laughter when she felt his tugs. Sometimes, he'd clamp his jaws firmly onto her sari, and then, when she stood up, she would feel him dangling behind her.

'Oho, silly fellow,' she would scold him. 'Eat your leaves, not my sari!'.

He stayed in the kitchen for as long as she was there, happily munching peels and scraps. He loved cabbage and *lauki* or bottle gourd peels. His absolute favourite, though, were green chillies. So many trades-men who had seen him over the years would laugh at the unusual pet, asking, 'Are you going to eat it? We have lots in our village.'

Eat?! The family was aghast. But, despite repeated requests, the tradespeople would not bring one back as a companion for Plod – carrying a live animal across a couple of days of hard travel seemed challenging. Finally, Samit decided to surprise Smita. He hoped it would bring her out of the lethargy she had sunk into. Usually very interested in her siblings' lives, she seemed to have withdrawn, much like the little tortoise.

Queries led him to reconnaissance the livestock market in the city. He came back wide-eyed at the variety of creatures available. There were tortoises aplenty! He carried Mr Plod there in a shoebox and learned that he was, in fact, a she! Oops, Miss Plod, not Mr! He finally chose an adventurous little soulmate for her, a sprightly fellow who clambered over the rest to get out of the cage. He loved his spirit, he said.

Smita would be in paroxysms of laughter over his mischief or shaking her head in despair. More oval than the rotund little Plod, he was also more agile and aggressive. He would push her out of the way and eat his meal and hers. He, too, learned to reach the kitchen and would snap at the maid's hands if he was not served immediately, often tumbling into the vegetables and trying to eat them whole. Plod shrank out of his way. She retreated into her shell and had to be coaxed to come out. This proved therapeutic for Smita, in a way, since she was shaken out of her languor to call out to Plod and encourage her to eat. Her bond grew stronger and closer.

Though she named them Mr. and Mrs. Plod, the new Mr. Plod was impatient and assertive. He wanted to explore his new terrain, to get under cupboards and investigate dark corners. He was often reluctantly pulled out with the back of the broom from odd hiding places. Nor was he interested in his bride, so the happy consummation never happened.

Smita tried to connect with the new Plod, but soon gave up and observed him from a distance. Gentle Miss Plod continued to hear her confidences and heartaches, as well as her travels to meet her siblings.

'Ploddy, I'm good at baking. When I feel very sad, I bake. Everyone loves my cakes. I feel so happy when people compliment me, especially Dad and my *Masi*.'

'And you know, now I'm learning to type. I just don't like to make a mistake, then I rip out the sheet of paper if even a full stop is incorrect.'

139

Plod heard about her bus rides to and from college, how she'd pick up pastries and medicines en route and bring everything back safely. She heard about her love and sympathy for a cousin who had developed such paranoia she would not exit her home and how Smita would visit her every month carrying *mishti* or sweets. Plod was her dearest and closest friend.

And then, one day, some 20 years since Miss Plod had come home, the unthinkable happened. She did not eat the food served to her. She hadn't seemed to have moved in a few hours. When Smita picked her up, her head hung loose. Her limbs splayed out when she turned upside down, but there was no further movement. Her eyes were shut.

'No! How could it be? Mom, don't tortoises live to a hundred or more? Please don't die, Ploddy,' she entreated. Eyes wide with dread, Smita went with Mom and took Plod to the vet. Unfortunately, he confirmed her worst fears. Smita was inconsolable. Silent tears poured down her cheeks.

The next day, the family walked to a nearby pond and quietly released old Plod. New Mr Plod seemed to notice her absence, too. He walked around the house and was found in unexpected places. It felt like he was looking for her. This shared feeling of loss and dislocation endeared him to Smita. She felt a bond with him, she'd never felt before. But, he was restless, not as placid and patient as the other one. He didn't want to be held and kissed or talked to. He wriggled and hopped out of her grasp. He was independent. He pumped his little legs till he flipped over if he fell on his back. It was hard to form a companionship with him.

Smita took a while to come to terms with Plod's passing. That silent, seemingly one-way friendship had meant more to her than anyone realised.

Note from author: This story draws from true events, with, of course, authorial licence to make it more engaging. Please keep in mind that it dates back to a time when tortoises and other such creatures could be domesticated, unlike the unfortunate situation today when many are endangered.

THE MOONLIT CLOUDS

SUMONA GHOSH DAS, USA

The sky was overcast with rain clouds as Raima pulled her car out of the garage. She was taking a short trip to the local grocery store to buy vegetables and spices for dinner that evening. Raima was at a stage in her life where she was a half-empty nester. One of her daughters was in college, and the other was in high school. Her life had been a kaleidoscope of different terrains—prairies, valleys, mountains, and cascading waterfalls. Raima was reminiscing about her life path when she entered the store. Deep in her thoughts, she picked up a few vine-ripened tomatoes, carefully selecting a fresh bunch of sixes, and put it in her basket.

Next, the evenly textured, bite-sized Yukon gold potatoes in plastic pouches caught her attention, triggering a landslide of recipes gushing through her overactive mind. She almost published a book of potato recipes, standing between the aisles of the vegetables and the meats section. Coming back to her senses and grasping the reality of life in the USA, she put a hold on her imaginary unpublished book. She settled on a recipe for a quintessential Bengali dish, *Aloo Posto*.

Raima reached the payment line and carefully put all the groceries on the conveyor belt. As she watched her beloved, perfectly round Yukon gold potatoes rolling towards the cashier, Raima was greeted by one of the brightest smiles she had ever seen on a person's face. Struck by her friendliness, Raima smiled back. The young cashier started scanning the items, one by one.

'Paper or plastic?' she asked. 'Paper bag, please!' Raima said. 'Will you make a delicious Indian curry with these potatoes?' she asked while scanning the bag. Pleasantly startled by her words, Raima said, 'Well, it would not be a curry but of a drier consistency.' Curious, Raima asked the girl, 'Which country are you from?' The girl said, 'I am from Afghanistan; my name is Badra!' Raima could not help but look at her face for the second time. She noted the jet-black hair tied neatly in a knot, a pair of curious big eyes, a small sharp nose, quaint lips that smiled and the flawless wheatish yellow skin tone. She was perhaps in her late 20s, Raima concluded.

'Hi, Badra. I am Raima,' she exclaimed. 'Did you arrive in the USA after the president pulled out the forces from Afghanistan?' 'Yes, I came two years ago. Life has been alright but challenging so far.' said Badra. Her fluency in English struck Raima. Badra was a well-educated Afghani girl who happened to be the victim of circumstances.

'What do you do?' asked Badra. 'I am a mental health counselor,' said Raima. 'Oh, that's wonderful. Can I contact you?' asked Badra. 'Sure, here is my number. I would like to hear about you,' said Raima. 'You promise you will not cry?' asked Badra. The words struck Raima like a bolt of thunder. 'I'll try,' she said with a passive smile.

Raima left the grocery store with mixed feelings and a heavy yet hopeful heart. The next few days were quite hectic for Raima as she got busy with social obligations, work, and family commitments. The following week, she got a surprise text from Badra, who wanted to meet and chat. Badra's text looked desperate. Raima second-guessed that she was reading too much into the text because of her preconceived bias of what life can bring to a refugee and an asylum seeker.

Raima met Badra at a coffee shop near the grocery store. She grabbed a coffee from the counter and anxiously waited for Badra on the corner sofa of the cafe, thinking about the text. 'I hope she is doing OK,' thought Raima. A few minutes later, Badra emerged from behind the sliding door. She was relieved that Raima had arrived. The women greeted each other with nods and a smile. Badra sat down with a chocolate chip butter cookie in her hand. 'This is a luxury for me, you know?' she said, pointing towards the cookie. 'How have you been?' asked Raima. 'I'm doing OK,' said Badra.

For the next hour and a half, Raima was drawn into the journey of a refugee girl from Afghanistan to the Middle East to Germany and, finally, to the USA. Badra's uncle and cousin got killed while trying to flee the war-hit areas of Afghanistan. Rescue flights were being sent from the USA. The fleeing families were competing against each other to get in line for immigration to board the flights. Unfortunately, Badra got caught in a stampede in one such fleeing episode. She could not get up after she was pushed to the ground. She lay there for almost three hours, half unconscious, bleeding from her uterus.

The stampede nearly crushed her body as she lay in a fetal position. She recollected later from her blurry memory that the foreign armed forces had picked her up and sent her to the nearest hospital. After getting initial treatment, the U.S. agency took her to Dubai. She was taken directly to a hospital for her deteriorating condition and heavy vaginal bleeding. After a few days, she was again sent to Frankfurt, Germany, for further treatment. Badra's uterine bleeding continued for months.

Raima listened to Badra with utmost attention and care. Humans of the developed country can never fathom these multiple layers of despair and loss of such magnitude. The thought humbled Raima. She felt like a tiny shell on the ocean shore, privileged to enjoy the sunrise but unaccustomed to the world of Badra, who was gasping for a life jacket in the dark depths of the

148

same ocean. Raima froze at the morbidity of this crude contrast.

The German officials processed Badra's passport and visa to migrate to the USA. Badra landed in the Land of the Free in March 2021 at an airport near the U.S. capital. She was transported to Texas soon after she landed in Washington, D.C. In a new country with a markedly different culture and new people, Badra feared being at the receiving end of Islamophobia that was gripping Western countries. She found herself in an existential crisis. She desperately looked for jobs that would put food on her plate at the end of the day. Her education in English had made this path attainable. There were impending challenges of personal safety, financial security, shelter, and even clothes. Badra lived in Texas for two years and worked as a public school student aide. She made minimum wage, which barely lasted her through the month.

Two years later, under the U.S. Government's Office of Refugee Resettlement (ORR), Badra was relocated to the Washington, D.C. metropolitan area. She found a basement apartment in one of the suburbs of Northern Virginia. She said that she missed her family back in Afghanistan. She had left behind her husband, parents, and two siblings. She had promised her husband that she would arrange for him to travel to the USA once she had settled down and established financial stability. She felt lonely and had no one to talk to after a long workday. While working three jobs, her tired mind wandered off to her hometown in Afghanistan, often thinking about her loved ones. Since she barely had the energy to prepare dinner after a long workday, she missed her mother's homemade food that her family would eat together. When she saw families with spouses and children, she missed her husband dearly, who never pressured Badra to wear a hijab or put any restrictions on her that are prevalent in Afghanistan.

Raima watched Badra's emotions while she talked about her apprehensions and doubts about whether she would be able to start a family in the future since she had this uterine trauma. Badra feared for her family's life back in her country. Now, under Taliban rule, her sisters were not allowed to go to school. Wearing a burqa was now enforced on all women under this regime. She was grateful to be in the USA but fearful of her loved ones' destiny back home. The counselor in Raima saw the tormented mind, hopelessness, helplessness, hurt and despair screaming through those big, beautiful eyes. Badra's sheer resilience and courage were shining through her indomitable heart.

Raima sensed that a steady income, health insurance, and a valid driver's license would put Badra on the path of acculturation in American society. Badra was working three jobs, which was quite tiring at the end of the day. She had health issues due to the physical trauma. Treatment was imperative, but she could not afford insurance. Raima promised to help her in the job search. She suggested to Badra to look for jobs in local public schools. She was multilingual and could speak Dari, some Pashto, and knew English as a second language. Badra could be an excellent resource for the multilingual community of immigrant children in the local public schools. Badra was quite excited about this idea and got to work on her resume the same night.

Raima was awakened by a jubilant text the following day. It was from Badra. 'I have submitted my resume to Solidarity High School! Do you think they will like my profile?' asked Badra. 'I have no doubt they will be quite impressed with your talent and calibre,' Raima said optimistically. 'Would you like to make an appointment with the Department of Motor Vehicle for your learner's permit and driving test?' Raima asked. 'Sure! I cannot wait to get a hold of my life and be independent! Thank you, Raima; I am grateful to you,' said Badra.

Such simple help received such extraordinary gratitude! Raima thought about entitlement in her present world and society. She compared her lifestyle, social connections, financial stability, well-resourced children, and the comfort of everyday life to the likes of Badra. She could not shake off the imposter syndrome that was bordering on guilt, a classic impairment of every counselor. Raima's conviction to help Badra grew stronger.

After waiting for a week, Badra called Raima. A disheartened voice said that she did not get the job. 'There is a great need for multilingual personnel in the USA, especially in counselling, healthcare, and education. You will find a stable job very soon; have faith in the process,' said Raima. For the next few days, both women went through the County's education website to find a suitable job placement for Badra. In the meantime, Raima investigated the driving licence procedure and health insurance catering towards the marginalised immigrant population. She researched how the USA provided legal asylum and eased the path of job search for refugees from war-hit countries. She gathered information for Badra so she could collect the necessary government permits. Sensing Badra's nervousness, Raima told her, 'I will take you to these offices, so do not worry; just have your papers ready.' Badra was relieved by Raima's assurance. 'Thank you so much. I am not sure how I can ever repay you.' Badra was in tears. 'Just live well and be happy; that will be my repayment.' Raima hugged her with a smile.

An interview call from Justice High School lifted Badra's spirits. Raima could hear her cheerful voice on the phone. The next day, Badra anxiously waited for Raima near the pavement of her basement apartment. Raima drove her to the county public school. 'I am nervous but excited; please wish me luck,' said an anxious Badra. 'You will be fine, and something tells me you will get the job,' said Raima with a smile. 'Really you think so?' asked Badra. 'Yes! And do not forget to tell them your story of survival and resilience and that you are multilingual. Talk about your experience with young kids; tell them something interesting that happened in the Texas school where you made an impact of some kind. The words from your resume will come alive when you tell those stories. The interviewer will better connect with you with your narrative.' Raima gave her two cents to boost Badra's self-confidence.

'OK, thanks! Those are great points; I will try my best,' Badra told Raima as she exited the car. Raima saw a fearless young girl walk towards the school's main door, confidently showing her identification card to the security camera, and go inside as the secretary buzzed her in. Raima saw some kids who were art teachers earnestly describing the grand Parthenon columns standing tall at the entrance. The columns gave a remarkable impression of old buildings typical of the Washington D.C. landscape.

'The interview went very well! I connected my story and its impact on my life with the questions they asked, just as you told me. Thank you so much! That last-minute pep talk helped.' Badra said in a content voice. 'People will be lucky to get an employee like you. You will be hired where you are needed the most. The universe will put the right kind of school and job in front of you, which is meant to be. However, I hope you will get this job,' Raima confidently said. The next few weeks were a waiting game.

'I got the job, Ms. Raima! I got the job, Ms. Raima! I am so happy. It is unbelievable. I got the job! They like me and say I am a good fit for the student body who relocated as refugees and immigrants and faced challenges in understanding English. I can be their interpreter, and I can also help them with spoken English. I can even help them with clerical work as needed. The school administration said I would get health insurance from the County, so there is no need to worry. Thank you so much. I don't know what I would do without you, Ms Raima.' Badra's jubilant young voice kept chirping on the phone. Raima could not hold back tears of joy. 'Congratulations, you made it Badra. You deserve this. You achieved your goal with hard work, perseverance, and resilience. Now it is time to rejoice,' said the elated Raima. The two women met at the coffee shop that witnessed the beginning of a new friendship. They celebrated Badra's new job with the warm, toasty comfort of perfectly brewed coffee and sweet, savoury, sinful strawberry croissants.

'What is the meaning of Raima?' asked Badra. 'It means love and kindness,' said Raima. 'It is a beautiful name,' said a smiling Badra. She continued, 'Badra means full moon in Arabic.' 'In my culture and language, Badra means rain clouds,' exclaimed Raima. The two women stared at each other, struck by how serendipity had brought them together; sensing each other's thoughts, they smiled. Raima met Badra at the grocery store on a rainy, cloudy day. That evening, the rain clouds dispersed and gave way to a full moon. This was the beginning of the journey of a refugee girl on new soil. The heartstrings keep pulling, and the pang of leaving the dearest ones back home does not cease. However, the spirit that refuses to give up, the mind that is smart, diligent, and bright, and a warm, adaptive, and kind personality is the embodiment of a woman named Badra.

Glossary

Aloo Posto: Famous comfort food of the people of eastern India, especially in Bengal, made with potatoes and poppy seed paste and cooked in mustard oil.
Badra: a name that means full moon in the Farsi language. It means rain clouds in the Hindi language in India.
Hijab: a scarf covering hair and neck as a modest attire for women in Islam religion.
Raima: a name that means love, kindness, compassion, and acceptance in Indian and Pakistani culture.

ONCE UPON A

HOLIDAY

SUJATHA MURTHY, INDIA

Contrary to their name, *Dak* bungalows were not just post-houses or rest stops when letters were delivered by horseback to different post offices during British rule in India. They also doubled up as travellers' bungalows during the British Raj, especially for government officials. They often stayed there, so care was taken to build and maintain them well. More than 78 years after Indian Independence, many still stand crumbling, deep inside forests and on top of misty mountains. Fighting time has had its effect, but they still have a hold over the minds of the people who are fond of and fascinated by them. Having read this, Neha exclaimed excitedly, 'Guys, this place called *Friend's Dak Bungalow* is perfect. It's right in the middle of the Bandipur forest. And it has fabulous reviews on Google.' Reema looked at her as Neha cleared her throat and continued, 'Listen to this - Ajit Kaka is unbelievable. He is an excellent cook and takes great care to ensure visitors have every comfort; the place is spotlessly clean, and the jungle walk was exciting.'

'Fine, fine, Neha, you book it online then, and we all will pay you our share,' Reema said, looking at the two boys who were absorbed in the cricket match on TV, even though it was on mute.

On Saturday morning, after a lovely road trip from Bangalore, they drove smoothly into the porch way of the *Dak* Bungalow. The exterior of the building was made of red brick, supported by white arches, and covered with beautiful hanging ivy. The grass was cut to the correct length, making the lawn look neat and manicured. Some of the bushes had been cut into shapes. 'Look, a peacock! And there's an elephant!' Reema and Neha were pretty excited. The boys whipped out their phones and took pictures of the girls with practised ease.

It was at this moment that the front door opened with a creak. And out stepped the caretaker of the house. He walked over slowly towards them, as if his joints were not quite in the mood to work. And greeting them cheerfully enough, he said in a soft, shaky voice, *'Aayiye, andar aayiye.'*

They entered the colonial-style living room with high ceilings, still furnished in the style of the old days. Oddly enough, everything was in pristine condition. Almost as if . . . new. But that was simply not possible now, was it? They followed the caretaker, Ajit Kaka, onto the grand wooden staircase that was polished like a mirror and checked into their rooms on the first floor. Both rooms had four-poster beds, carved dressers and ceiling fans hanging high above. The bathrooms were gorgeously large, with bathtubs and double basins. Once Kaka had placed their luggage in the rooms, he turned to leave. Karan said, 'Uhh Kaka, are there any other people staying here?'

Kaka thought momentarily, then shook his head. 'No, it's just me. And now all of you.'

Sam couldn't help himself and cut in, 'Kaka, we are very hungry. May we have lunch soon?'

Kaka turned to look at him. The decades that had passed had rendered his eyes almost colourless. He stood thinking for a few minutes, and just as the silence was getting uncomfortable, he said slowly, 'Let me go and see what I can rustle up quickly. Come down after you freshen up.'

Half an hour later, the four approached the dining table. Just then, Kaka walked in from the kitchen at the far end of the corridor, carefully balancing a beautiful platter in his hand. As he approached them, Neha looked puzzled and said softly to Sam, 'Doesn't he seem different somehow?'

Kaka was walking strangely with a feminine gait, showing no sign of stiff joints. He approached them and set the platter in the centre of the already laden table. Then, with a bright smile, he lifted the lid off each dish, calling out, 'Mulligatawny soup, Devilled eggs, balti vegetables, coronation chicken and … sherry trifle pudding!'

As the four guests gasped at the gorgeous dessert on display, their focus was back firmly on the food. Neha looked confused, she wanted to say that she hadn't really heard of these dishes; they sounded like they were straight out of the earlier century! But then she saw that the others were busy taking pictures for Instagram and kept it to herself. Selfies abounded with the sherry trifle pudding. Then they tucked in heartily. The food was absolutely outstanding. Kaka stood watching them shyly, unmindfully twisting and un-twisting the end of the *gamcha* hanging over his shoul-der. Later that evening, Kaka got a bonfire ready for them. As the girls and boys sang along to the latest songs and danced, he watched them from the porch, sitting on an old-world planter's chair and smoking. Karan went up to him with his Vape to tell him that it was quite cool that Kaka had a similar one. With a loud booming laugh, completely unexpected from his frail frame, Kaka showed him the British Raj-era pipe in his hand and the quaint leather pouch for his tobacco and explained how it worked. Karan stood dumbstruck as did the others until finally Neha managed to say in a shaky voice that it was time to sleep. Kaka replied in a clipped British accent and perfect English, 'Yes, yes, goodnight, my dearies. I will see you at 7 a.m. sharp when we head out for the jungle walk. We'll be back here for tea and breakfast, don't you worry.' And up he stood, then walked, no, marched away.

Neha and Reema clutched each other tightly. Karan's face had gone white. Sam put his arm around the girls protectively. Kaka was different again.

Back in Reema's room, they spoke in hushed whispers. Things didn't seem quite right. What should they do now? Kaka didn't seem like he meant them any harm. But they would be leaving at lunchtime tomorrow anyway, would they not? If they stayed alert and kept together, they would be okay. And so, having calmed down, they slept fitfully through the night. Not without locking the doors well, though.

Meanwhile, far away from the main house, in the back room of the servant's quarters of the *Dak* Bungalow, things were not so quiet. Kaka sat on his bed, looking a bit upset. In broken English interspersed with Hindi, he said to the shimmering apparition sitting next to him on the bed, 'How many times I have to tell you Saheb, you don't have to do all this anymore.'

165

The apparition guffawed loudly, putting an arm over Kaka's frail shoulder, and said in a clipped British accent, 'It's entirely my pleasure, Ajit. Your guests are my guests, too!'

From above, a woman's soft voice whispered, 'Kaka, we are in this together. We are happy to help you, *khushi khushi kartey hain*!' Kaka looked up at the dark shadow squatting lightly on the ceiling fan, with waist-length hair hanging over its shoulder and two yellow eyes glittering from deep within.

He smiled and said, 'Oh, there you are, Seeta. Cooking such fancy stuff …

pudding and all, what if they had suspected something is not right, huh?'

The dark form jumped onto the wall and slid down in front of Kaka with a shrieking, unearthly laugh. Then it said, 'Sorry, Kaka, my old habits won't leave me, even if I have left your world. I like to show off my skills so they can take pictures of my cooking on those lit-up rectangles they like to hold ... oh, I just love it!'

The ghost of the Saheb laughed, and Kaka smiled indulgently as he said, 'Mobile phone, *Pagli,* that's what it is.' Kaka sighed and said, 'What I'm saying is that both of you are doing all my work, and I rest all day. Even my own family won't do so much!'

'It's because of you that we get to enjoy our afterlife,' said the ghost of the *Saheb.* 'What matters is that our *Dak* Bungalow stays popular, and your job is safe forever.'

'Yes,' the ghost of Sita agreed. 'When you first began to see and hear us 50 years ago, you didn't get scared. You not only accepted and comforted us, but allowed us to stay here peacefully with you and became our friend. And so, we shall stay ... friends forever.' She held out her black disembodied hand, on which was then placed a pale, shimmering, see-through hand. Kaka smiled and placed his hand on theirs. These two could be so childish sometimes.

The next morning, the girls and boys kept close during the jungle walk. Kaka was the same as last night, speaking perfect British-era English. He knew the jungle inside out, pointing out the songbirds, interesting flora and fauna, and even a Pitcher Plant. He spoke of hunts and army camps during the Raj, making the whole experience alive. Despite themselves, the young ones couldn't help but ask questions and enjoy the walk. Breakfast was ready when they came back to the *Dak* Bungalow.

Karan and Sam looked at each other. Kaka, the caretaker here, was the only other person in the *Dak* Bungalow, and he had accompanied them on the jungle walk. Then who had set up this outdoor breakfast table with its red checked cloth, plates full of buttered toast, bowls of fruits, hot tea and biscuits?

Thinking that it was better not to ask, they all ate well. Then, quickly packing their bags, they decided to leave early. Instead of checking out at lunchtime, they would head back now. As they loaded their luggage into their car, Kaka came out. He exclaimed, 'What's the hurry, chaps? Do stay a while longer.'

Sam said with a nervous smile, 'We would love to, Kaka, but it's a long drive back, and we want to go slowly and carefully.' Kaka thought over this and nodded, 'Hmm. That would be the right thing to do, yes. Well, I hope you enjoyed your visit. And remember to give us a great review on . . . what it is called . . . umm . . he racked his brains, his forehead wrinkling as he thought hard.

Karan said, 'Google?'

Kaka's face brightened, 'Yes, good lad, that's the one.' As the other smiled, Neha said, 'Of course, we will rate this bungalow and you, a full 5 stars, Kaka. Thank you, we had a lovely stay!'

169

As the car drove away from the porch, Reema turned back to see Kaka waving happily. Then he turned, hands clasped behind his straight back and marched back into the *Dak* Bungalow. On the first-floor window, in the very room they had slept in, a dark shadow seemed to shimmer across, holding a duster. Was it cleaning up after them? Reema shook her head, unable to believe what she saw. Was the Friend's *Dak* Bungalow stay an experience to remember? She'd say it was. One day, maybe she would tell her children and grand-children all that she'd seen and heard - once upon a holiday.

Glossary

Aayiye, andar aayiye: do come in.

Khushi khushi kartey hain: we do it happily.

Gamcha: a traditional coarse cotton cloth, often worn on one side of the shoulder and used as a hanky or towel for personal use, such as wiping the face or hands.

Pagli: a fond way to call someone childlike/ straightforward.

AROUND THE CORNER

REJINA SADHU, SWITZERLAND

It had been a long time since they had met. They seemed destined to meet at the end of a staircase or around the corner. In the misty, foggy realms, the little girl skipping through the corridor with a line of tiny homes interacted with everyone there.

'Rani, are you there?' The nudge from Deepak, her husband, brought her back to the present.

Rani shook her head to clear up her thoughts. When the world around encroached on her, she took refuge in the corridors of her past. Deepak had given her yet another dose of how he had married a nincompoop with no superlative skills. Rani struggled with this onslaught of negativity every day. Her life before getting married seemed so distant. With a big sigh, she turned her attention to Deepak.

They were going to her in-laws' place for the summer break. Deepak's parents and siblings lived in a large town towards the north. He usually spent a few days with his parents and siblings who lived in the same city and then spent the rest of his holiday arranging trips for the whole family to travel to his dream destinations. Holidays tended to leave her exhausted due to the constant pressure of catering to everyone's comfort and needs.

Her in-laws supported Rani in everything as long as her priority was her family. Things that did not benefit the kids or Deepak directly were considered unnecessary. The stories stayed unwritten, the rhythms in her soul stayed unsung, and the colours in her brushes stayed unpainted. She had been unable to emphasise her need for space or time and her need to do something for herself over the last decades. She felt like an impostor living a life choreographed by others. Having no confidante for her innermost thoughts made her lonely. Loyalty to her family competed with her need to confide. Maintaining her calm was becoming more challenging when everything around her threatened to battle her composure.

Rani felt overwhelmed by the demands of her career, family and the fast-paced world. Her only solace was when SHE appeared before her. Rani could see her picking up a baby, patting him, singing a rhyme, coaxing a smile and then moving on to the next home. The smile on the elderly lady's face as she narrated her day's routine to her was numinous. As she pushed ahead, a lady from the neighbouring home rushed forward with a bowl and a spoon, urging her to taste her new dish. Rani saw her relishing the treat and complimenting the lady in her mind's eye. As She walked towards her home, stopping here and there to chat with everyone, Rani's thoughts accompanied the vision. her agitated heart calmed down and warmed up a little. Rani once again pasted a smile on her face and turned to encounter the universe. Deepak and the world might try to topple her dreams, but Rani had her.

Rani always came through as a gregarious, youthful and loving spirit, but she could not have nurtured her indomitable spirit without her. When a particular aroma or a written or spoken word conjured a wave of loneliness or yearning for someone of her own, Rani turned around the corner and tried to meet her.

'How can even such a small thing not be comprehended by your small brain? You cannot understand the intricacies of culture or wisdom. The kids are picking on your erroneous messages and are being negatively impacted,' shouted Deepak. Rani curbed the urge to lash out as she knew it was futile. Her voice was helpful when it was convenient for

Deepak and supported his ambitions and dreams. Everything else was superfluous.

Deepak's reproach had just dampened her sparkle of life, but SHE was the one ray of light that still brought a glow to Rani's life and kept her moving forward. Like other times, today, SHE zoned off and searched her heart. SHE met her down the staircase and around the corner. SHE looked at Rani and beckoned her.

Suddenly, an old grandma appeared behind her and asked whether she was alright in Marathi: '*Kashi aches? Bari aahsnaa?*' Time and distance compressed and converged to that moment. Rani stopped and questioned herself, 'Am I okay?' Whenever she had a discernible moment, whether happy or not, SHE was the only one she could share it with without any restraint.

Rani walked down memory lane, revisiting the dreams and aspirations of her childhood whenever she met her. She remembered the joy of exploring new ideas, the excitement of learning something new, and the boundless optimism that filled her heart. As she reconnected with her younger self, she realised that the key to regaining her positivity lay in embracing those simple pleasures and being grateful for the love and affection that the ones in her past had bestowed on her.

On a phone call with her mother, aunt or neighbour, they expressed their pride in knowing her and being part of her life. Tears of humility and self-acceptance boosted Rani's declining self-esteem. By allowing herself to dream significantly and approach challenges with the same enthusiasm as a child, Rani discovered a renewed sense of purpose and a deeper understanding of her true potential. This journey back to her roots brought her joy and provided valuable insights that helped her navigate her present with confidence and grace.

176

Above all, her younger self, who was ready to meet her around the corner, share her innermost thoughts, and hold her hand through thick and thin, was her greatest blessing.

Glossary

Kashi ashes: How are you in Marathi.
Bari aahes, naa: You are all right in Marathi.

THE CIRCLE

OF LIFE

BRINDARICA BOSE, SWITZERLAND

The pandemic had hit.

It was August 2020, and COVID-19 had taken its toll—first, among unknowns reported in the news, then within my circle of acquaintances, and finally within my family.

I was travelling from Frankfurt Airport to Kolkata, transit via New Delhi.

As I made my way toward the lounge at New Delhi Airport, I encountered a young man named Namman from the airport services, who my husband had appointed to guide me during transit. He wore a crisp blue suit and a flimsy blue mask. His neatly gelled hair and thick lashes that framed dark, expressive eyes, sparked confidence in him. Surprisingly, he guided me through passport control and luggage checks with remarkable efficiency, bypassing the long lines filled with newly arrived passengers from the UAE.

I was in a complete daze, and my mind was in a turmoil. I wore a kurta and jeans. A protective mask similar to a gas mask obscured my face, and thick plastic glasses completely covered my eyes. The rubber bands of which pressed against my temples, but I dared not remove them. I wanted to ensure that the virus could enter from nowhere.

Following Namman, somehow eased my anxiety. He seemed so much more normal compared to my surroundings and in contrast to the unfamiliar reflection (of myself) that I glimpsed, as we walked towards the airport lounge. At the entrance, of the lounge, Namman exchanged a few words with the receptionist and then, in his calm, reassuring tone, dropped my handbag near the entrance. He encouraged me to rest, and promised to return for my connecting flight to Kolkata in three hours.

My glasses were fogged up, partly from my nervous breathing and partly from perspiration. The air conditioning (AC) had been deliberately turned off due to circulation of the air (and the virus). I noticed it was a small, dimly lit room. There were restrictions on the number of people allowed inside. It was the end of August, pretty humid in New Delhi. To add to it, there was an eerie silence enveloping the room. Only six travellers occupied the space.

I chose a chair near the entrance, placed my handbag beside me, and sat down after applying hand-sanitiser. Two couples were absorbed in their phones and laptops, occupying the same room. The dim light felt inadequate, so I asked the receptionist to improve the lighting. She informed me that it was night, and the lights had to remain dimmed. I let it go; I felt like, I had limited energy and breathing air, and didn't want to waste it on a debate. I returned to my seat, trying to rest for the next two hours, but instead, felt compelled to walk outside the lounge. There was a restlessness I couldn't get rid of, since the beginning of my journey. Barriers outside, blocked my way everywhere. Some passengers were sprawled on seats, police were guarding entrances, and the invisible threat of the virus was everywhere. How to fight an invisible enemy?

After a while, I had no choice but to retreat to the dimly lit lounge. Sometimes, when the mind becomes numb, you need someone to provide a sense of routine, or guide. Perhaps an invisible force was assisting me? Sending me messages through the movies I watched on the flight, telling me what to do next. I was still sorting out my thoughts, emotions, memories, and things to do. I had no room for ´panic´ to enter my mind. What was done was done. Thankfully, after almost two hours, the receptionist announced that our breakfast would soon be served. We all removed our masks, and for the first time, I saw the faces of my fellow passengers waiting with me in the lounge.

We maintained our distance, aware that with our masks off, the risk had increased. But we had all tested negative and completed a mountain of paperwork to be allowed to travel, so we wouldn't infect each other inside that room.

Hot *idlis* with my favourite coconut *chutney* and thick *sambhar* were served, accompanied by tea in earthen cups. Tears pricked my eyes as I broke off a piece of the soft *idli* and dipped it in the *sambhar*. Was it relief or an involuntary reaction? Regardless, I ate hungrily and finished quickly. After re-sanitizing my hands, I wrapped my fingers around the earthen cup and consciously observed my fellow passengers.

One woman had stepped outside, phone in hand, instructing her son about what was stocked in the fridge. She was Indian but spoke English with an American accent.

Next to her, was a young couple, engaged in a back-and-forth conversation—with the man urging the woman to rest, and the woman giving her reasons, why she didn't want to. The young woman, half-reclining, dropped her legs on the table awkwardly. Despite the dim light, she was reading a book without any break. While sipping my tea, I felt compelled to break the silence. 'What book are you reading?' I asked her.

Everyone turned to look at me.

In the past two hours, we had not spoken with each other.

The young woman set her book down and replied, 'It's Khaled Hosseini's *A Thousand Splendid Suns*. I couldn't help but say, almost maternally, 'But it's so dark here! Do you want me to ask the receptionist to turn on the lights?' The young woman smiled and

183

replied, 'I didn't want to disturb anyone, actually. I can read in this light, too, and the book is so interesting, can't stop reading!'

Curious, I asked, 'What brings you here, if I may ask?' The young woman had barely touched her food, but now she toyed with it, smiling as she explained in a very calm voice, not at all anxious, instead laced with conviction.

'We want our child to be born in India. We're headed to my village in Andhra Pradesh, where my husband's family also lives.'

That explained her awkward posture and the gentle, caring reprimands her husband had been giving her for the last two hours.

The husband chimed in, 'We are leaving the USA for good. I've worked there as an IT engineer for almost five years, but we want to raise our family in India now. My wife is pregnant—she's in her sixth month, nearly her seventh. After this, they won't allow us to travel. He continued. 'We had long decided to return to India and raise our child there. We have big families, all living under the same roof, and we miss that environment in the USA, I will drop my wife in India, and then return to the USA to wrap up some formalities and return to India again, hopefully before the birth.'

I was surprised by what they said but didn't want to pry further. I congratulated them instead.

At that moment, the other couple in the room—the woman who had just returned from a trip to the ladies' room—interjected, 'Oh, we're from the USA too, East coast. Congratulations to both of you!' She smiled, tucking her mobile phone in her handbag. 'We're on our way to visit Appa.'

'We received a call two days ago that dad had developed a fever.' She paused, gathering her thoughts before continuing. 'My brother and I left everything and booked our tickets quickly.' She glanced at her brother and added, 'We have lived in the USA for over two decades. We have cousins who stay near our parent´s house. Last week it was my cousin who called. Appa has crossed 80, so we just hope …' Her voice trailed off, with a slight shift in her expressions. They both looked apprehensive—busy making calls to their office, homes in India and to the USA, alternating between Tamil and English, two parallel worlds in which most expats live. As I watched them finish breakfast, the older sister took the plates away and returned with two cups of coffee.

Meanwhile, the pregnant woman and her husband were wrapping up their meal. Her husband poured himself an extra cup of tea from the thermos kept inside our room, and asked if I wanted an extra cup as well. We still hadn't put on our masks. I nodded, and as he poured the piping hot tea, tears welled in my eyes—perhaps an involuntary reaction to the moment's warmth. He gently set my earthen cup on the glass table beside me, and settled back near his wife, close to the wall.

The last hour passed quickly, and soon, Namman returned to escort me to my domestic flight. I adjusted my special glasses and mask, ensuring my phone and extra masks were in place, and the small sanitizer liquid I was carrying everywhere.

Before I left, the pregnant woman looked up with a warm smile, and said, 'I wish you a good flight. Take care, *didi*, you will be fine.'

It felt as if she sensed that I was travelling to India for my father's final rites, who had passed away suddenly, but peacefully, a week ago. Maybe the unborn and the deceased had conspired somewhere in between, creating an unusual, momentary relationship—to send me another message—to live life without fear.

This, brief encounter with the travelers whom I met in transit, and the unusual circumstances that brought us together—sickness, death, and birth—stayed etched in my memory since then. It was a message to reconfirm the circle of life, the journey continues.

CONTRIBUTORS' PROFILES

The Editors and Coordinators

Ms. Debaleena Mukherjee, India *(Editor)*

 Debaleena is an author and a home-maker. She has published two books: *Ink-Smudged Dreams by the Reading Light* (poems) and *Coffee, Smiles, and Tears by Starlight* (short stories). She completed her M.Phil. from Jadavpur University. Reading and writing are her way of life. She loves all genres and reads even newspaper packets. She has a little library at home—sitting in her favourite recliner, holding a cup of coffee, a book, and her dreams.

SHE Connects

Dr. Rejina Sadhu, Switzerland (*Editor*)

Dr Rejina Sadhu is a neurobiologist working in the pharmaceutical industry and an author and editor with the *She Writers'* group. Passionate about diversity, equity and inclusion, she co-leads an employee resource group for working parents. A Malayali born in Mumbai, she moved to Switzerland for her PhD, got married to a Bengali and continued to explore the world through books, travel, music and food with her family. She speaks five languages fluently and started writing poems and stories at a young age for her school magazine and moved on to publish in university publications. The organisers of the Bombay Hindi Sahitya Parishad published her Hindi poems, which she read at their annual event. Her scientific essays earned critical acclaim from the Nobel Laureate Harold Kroto. Art, culture, people, books and food are her mainstays.

Ms. Saleha Singh, Australia (*Editor, Copyeditor*)

Saleha, a Communications professional, has called Melbourne home since 2004 and has been associated with SHE since 2021. Saleha is passionate about the community and considers herself a ripple in the ocean, trying to bring awareness, acceptance, and education. She founded Chai, Chat & Community, a weekly webcast that discusses swept-under-the-carpet South Asian issues. She is the co-chair of the Multicultural Women's Alliance Against Family Violence and

189

she is on the board of IndianCare, a not-for-profit community organisation.

Dr. Teesta Ghosh, USA (*Editor-in-Chief*)

Teesta is an academic by profession and lives with her family in the Washington, DC, area. She led an itinerant life living in different parts of India in her childhood and considers that experience profoundly influenced in shaping her world-view. Subsequently, she moved to the USA to pursue her doctoral studies. Outside the classroom, she was a manager for her son's soccer team, judged debate competitions, and was a member of a book club devoted to child pedagogy. She enjoys travelling, is a nature enthusiast, loves cooking, and considers herself a writer by accident rather than design. She abides by the motto: be human, be humane.

Dr. Vinita Godinho, Australia (*Chief-Coordinator*)

Vinita was born and brought up in Kolkata and now lives in Australia. She has worn many hats in her professional life—NGO executive, banker, academic and business owner—but is proudest of her role as the mother of two boys. Vinita loves music, keeping fit, staying in touch with friends and family, and travelling. Currently balancing work with further study, she hopes to keep sharing her experiences by finding the time to keep up with her writing.

SHE Connects

Bidisha Chakraborti, USA *(Coordinator)*

Bidisha is a professional specialized in the Insurance industry for a large consulting firm. Born in a Bengali family, brought up in Chandigarh and married to a Tamilian, blended cultures (and kitchens!) make her feel at home. Outside of her day job as a researcher, she likes to find time to travel with her husband. Despite being a novice storyteller, her interest in writing comes from middle school days where two of her closest friends had encouraged her to 'put pen to her thoughts'.

Dr. Abhilasha Kumar, Switzerland *(Advisory Editor)*

Abhilasha is a researcher interested in various subjects, including astronomy, the occult, nature, and wildlife conservation. She is currently based in Basel, Switzerland, where she works in medical communication and is a mother to two boys. Exploring both the inner and outer worlds, Abhilasha enjoys photography, travelling, and writing as a means of self-discovery. She is a contributing author and co-editor for the *SHE Writers* anthologies, and you can follow her on Instagram @abhilashasudhirkumar.

191

Ms. Brindarica Bose, Switzerland *(Publisher, Advisory Editor)*

Brindarica studied science, business administration and fine arts. She is an artist and works part-time as an art teacher and as a Publications & Communications Manager at an international association. An ex-Times of India (Mumbai) employee, she has worked in print media for the last two decades. Her first book of short stories, *Swiss Masala*, was published in 2018; thereafter, she initiated the *SHE* anthology series with other authors. She lives in Switzerland with her family and founded Bose Creative Publishers (BCP) in 2020. Brindarica volunteers actively for Robin Hood Academy (India) and at Refugee centres in Wohlen, teaching art. She strongly believes in creative activism.

IG: @artistbrinda.@bose.creative.publishers

Ms. Sumona Ghosh Das, USA *(Advisory Editor)*

Sumona has been associated with the SHE group of authors since its inception in 2018. She is from Ranchi, India, and lives in the USA with her entrepreneur husband and two daughters. She passionately pursues her love for poetry, music, and writing. Sumona draws inspiration from the philosophies of Tagore, Carl Sagan, Alfred Adler and the likes of Pema Chödrön. Her writings found space in books and journals over a few decades.

Sumona is a Clinical Mental Health Counselor in training, and she aspires to help children, women of color, and immigrant and refugee populations. She is involved with various nonprofits in the Washington DC Metro area that support people from marginalised communities.

Sumona is an occasional blogger who writes about her lived experiences at www.sumonasworld.blogspot.com.

Writers and Volunteers

Ms. Radhika Singh, India

 Radhika has a postgraduate degree in Public Administration and has had a long and productive career in the cultural relations sector. She enjoys mentoring young adults and supporting their career aspirations. Radhika is passionate about protecting stray animals and looking after the homeless elderly. She is an honorary advisor to several civil society organisations that work in these sectors. She has recently set up a foundation to help underprivileged students access funding for higher education. She lives in Kolkata with her husband NK, her father, two rescued dogs and one bald bird. Her home serves as a transit space for injured strays, and the hosts keep falling madly in love with the guests, resulting in periodic heartbreak and tears. Radhika is a prolific writer whose stories are based on real-life experiences and incidents.

Dr. Jesleen Gill Papneja, *USA*

Jesleen lives in Virginia, USA, with her husband and two children. A dentist and consultant by profession, Jesleen is a red wine and champagne enthusiast. She is an ardent reader who loves to read all genres, from Enid Blyton to Khalil Gibran. Theatre is her undying passion; she has also been a Bollywood dance instructor. More spiritual than religious, Jesleen loves life and lives by the mantra, "Life is too short for unfinished business—when there is a lesson to be learned, learn it and move on."

Dr. Kanchana Singha Boseroy, *USA*

Kanchana is, by profession, a Developmental-Behavioral Pediatrician working with children with Neuro-developmental Disabilities. She is passionate about social justice and active in advocacy. Besides the USA, she works in several other countries with non-profit organisations. Being artistic, she has used Art in Medicine and has written poetry and many articles in her field. She has three grown-up children, a daughter-in-law and two granddaughters, several bonus children and grandchildren, all of whom make her life a joy-this big blended family. She resides in beautiful southern California with her husband and dog, continuing to read voraciously, write, do artwork, dance and live life to the fullest.

Ms. Riti Mukherjee, *Switzerland*

Born and raised in Kolkata, Riti Mukherjee moved to Switzerland in 2001 as an English Teacher and now runs her Language school in Baden. She has taught schoolchildren on three different continents and cultures, and life has given her that opportunity in India, America, and Europe. Art and Writing have been an integral part of her profession. She loves travelling and continues to sing and dance Indian classical. She believes in motherhood and the deeper, finer emotions that connect humanity and families, and she often expresses herself on social media. A writer, dancer, teacher, and entrepreneur who believes in miracles.

Ms. Shukla Lal, *India*

Since catching the literary bug on her 80th birthday, Shukla has written two historical romance sagas: Floating Logs, set in Kolkata (published by Notion Press in December 2019), and Rano and Phulo, set in undivided and then partitioned India (published by Goya Publishing in March 2019), and a collection of poems, Meri Nazmon ka Ehsaas, all captured on her iPad. She has completed the first draft of her third historical novel, Soul's Rapture, a mystical romance set in Lahore and Mumbai. Her deep spiritual practice and sense of wonder for the beauty of the world around her find expression in her storytelling. Her own lived experience adds lustre and authenticity to her stories.

www.authorat80.com. FB: Shukla Lal.

Ms. Sonia Kullar, *India*

Sonia Kullar is at once an ideator, educator, artist, author, mother, and daughter, balancing several roles with elan. Drawn to empowering women, she worked with girls who were first-generation learners, thus launching a substantial career as an educationist, teaching across ages and in some of India's best schools. She continues guiding and mentoring schools and teachers and writing texts that include stories of women achievers. She has now launched her label of original paintings and objets d'art, ASK.Art by Sonia Kullar. www.soniakullar.com. IG: kullarsoniaart FB: ASK.Art by Sonia Kullar

Ms. Sreyoshi Guha, *India (Volunteer, Social media)*

Sreyoshi was born and brought up in Kolkata. Loreto house, Middleton Row, is her alma mater. Nursery through to college this was her home away from home. After bringing up her two girls, she returned to teaching and training at Inlingua, New Delhi and then moved on to corporate training, communications and soft skills. She loves feeding people, cooking and baking. Dancing, which used to be her passion, took backstage. She loves writing short stories, mostly with interpretation left to the reader. With encouragement from her virtual and real

196

friends, she published her compilation of tiny tales titled 'Twilight Musings'.

Ms. Sujatha Murthy, *India*

 A storyteller of another sort, Sujatha is a creative director with more than two decades of brand building experience in the advertising world. She is also a mental health counsellor with a nuanced understanding of people's psychology and behaviour. Her experience working with and for people across geographies, cultures and mindsets finds expression in her writing - where truth melts into fiction. An avid traveller, she enjoys exploring and observing nature, culture, history and life across the length and breadth of the country. Sujatha currently lives and works in Bangalore, India.

SHE Connects

The Work Process Behind SHE books

The editors and coordinators of the SHE series are volunteers who share their precious time and expertise throughout the year to edit and interact with writers to improve their stories. It is a creative process that they happily engage in despite their limited time at their day jobs and personal engagements. The SHE writers and volunteers believe in bringing positive change in the lives of the underprivileged with their 'creative activism'.

The writers themselves do the work involved in producing the book. Many volunteer as editors, coordinators and publicists. The editors review the stories, the coordinators liaise between the editors and the writers, and the communication team manages the media outreach. The work is coordinated from conception to publication through a WhatsApp portal called the 'Female Voice.' Writers spread across many countries and time zones discuss, receive instructions and exchange information about the publication process using this portal.

If you wish to volunteer for SHE or are interested in writing fiction, write to us at bosecreativepubishers@gmail.com or contact one of the Editors or Coordinators with a sample of your writing and a short statement of motivation.

Profits from book sales get donated to support the underprivileged. We encourage our readers to get involved. Thank you for your help and support, hope you enjoyed reading this book.

BOSE CREATIVE PUBLISHERS

www.bosecreativepublishers.ch

Bose Creative Publishers, established in 2020 in Switzerland, is a collaborative publishing company that encourages writers and artists to publish a book together. All books are available at major online portals:

Fifteen travellers have come together to write this book of anecdotes and essays from their recent travels worldwide. From ship voyages to fishing in Alaska to visiting India's ancient forts and walls to reach the ends of the world at both poles. This book is unique when you read the stories shared across Alaska, Argentina, Armenia, Italy, France, India, Mexico, South Africa, Turkey, and Indonesia. Grab a copy of the book before your holidays!

Seven global social entrepreneurs (founders and leaders) share their advice. This book features seven founders of social enterprises from India, Switzerland, South Africa and the US. With case studies and interviews, this book talks about how and why these leaders started their social projects and how we, as a community, can support such causes. It talks about projects to support textiles from conflict zones, educate the underprivileged, or empower women with handicrafts and skills.

Authentic recipes from 16 Indian grandmas and their families. Published in 2021, this book features 25 authentic regional delicacies from 16 grandmas across India. Conceptualised by Mrs Debjani Dutta (a grandma herself), it includes recipes from grandmas who are 70 to 95 years old and live in various parts of India. It also provides legacy recipes passed on by family members. During the pandemic, the collaborators assembled this book in almost two years.

This book contains 43 flash fiction stories. Written by 22 women, it follows the journey of the river Ganga, with female protagonists experiencing different stages of life in 43 micro-stories. The book starts with a story set in Kilimanjaro and ends with a story set in the mother's womb.

This book is a memoir written by Prof. J. Bhattacharyya, US, and his search for a home, describing his journey from early childhood when he had to leave his home in Sherpur as an immigrant and travel to Kolkata during the partition. Then, he went to Delhi, later travelling to Brussels and settling in the US. With hilarious stand-alone chapters and stories lined with the pain of separation from home, family and friends, Expats and immigrants will connect with this book immediately.

Five Swiss artists share their urban sketches and paintings worldwide, including Switzerland. The paintings range from hotel rooms in Australia to skyline sketches from New York. This book, which is in colour and has two sections (world Travels and Switzerland), takes you worldwide with anecdotes and sketching tips and encourages you to pick up a paper and pencil and indulge in a drawing experience.

The stories in 'She Shines' are like myriad precious stones in a necklace, strung together through a common thread, yet each stone has a shape and colour. This common thread is resilience. The female gender throughout cultures, and perhaps through her unique feminine stance, has borne the brunt of many impossible circumstances. Yet, within her, certain persistence and forbearance can turn things around. Stories of resilience and victory are seasoned with two different flavours - the real and the surreal.

This book features India. The authors also include 21 short stories based on 21 Indian festivals, showcasing India's rich cultural heritage. Wherever we live, we keep these traditions close to our hearts. Each story ends with a festive recipe and an illustration. The festivals include Lohri, Eid, Durga Puja, Christmas, and many exotic festivals from all parts of India. This book also has small festive drawings after each story.

This book, a collection of poems by women of Indian origin, explores a potpourri of emotions. Our poets discuss fleeting moments, impressions, and perceptions in poems. Written by women from different professional backgrounds, this book is a delight and a gift to poetry lovers.

This is a collection of anecdotes from personal business trips worldwide, covering all the good, the odd, and the funny situations that can occur on railways, in hotels, in all-weather situations, in restaurants, and research institutes. The period here is at least twenty years old, so things have changed, and city infrastructures are different today.

**The Adventures
of Appa**

The short stories in this book offer a glimpse into how women have navigated their everyday lives and work. They appear in distinct roles, sometimes as trailblazers and at other times as innovators and facilitators. They are determined to fight discrimination in the workplace by acts of revolt that shatter the status quo.

Ganesh Murthy (Appa) is the protagonist of this book, born exactly one month after India gained independence from British rule. As the second of five siblings and the eldest son, he spent his early childhood in the serene landscapes of Kerala with his doting grandparents. This book is a collection of some of the tales laced with humour. Yet, beneath the humour lies the poignant story of a child who faced fear and trauma, a child who had to mature far too quickly, and whose dreams were dashed before they could fully form.

Thank you readers!

Thank you for reading this book and supporting us in the 'Books for a Cause' project. Please post your review on our online portals and recommend this book to your friends and family. Proceedings from the SHE books sales are donated to various charitable institutions. Editors, authors, and publisher volunteer their time and expertise to tell stories and run the SHE books project to give a creative platform to voices less heard. By reading this book, you are contributing to this good cause. Refer to other books published by the SHE group of writers: She Speaks (2019), She Celebrates (2020), She Reflects (2021), She Shines (2022), She Seeks (2023), She Achieves (2024), and She Connects (2025), available on online portals.

www.bosecreativepublishers.ch

Made in the USA
Middletown, DE
08 March 2025

72401645R00120